D1125239

THE AMERICAN TRUTH

The American Truth

A Novel

The American Truth

A Novel

A Nick Shelton Project

Mill City Press, Inc.

The Facts

Information the U.S. government does not want you to know.

The following section portrays proven facts and reliable evidence about the September 11th terrorist attacks. Up to this point, this information has been withheld from the American public.

Before reading the novel, it will help to read this nonfiction section to better understand the controversies surrounding the 9/11 terrorist attacks.

Author's Note: I recommend you read the expanded version of this section on this book's website (as opposed to following section in this book). The online version has interactive links and a bibliography that allows you to gain additional information. Also, I'm constantly correcting/updating this section online in order to provide the most accurate information possible.

www.AmTruth.com

Percent of Americans according to a recent survey who believe that it is "very likely" or "somewhat likely" that government officials either allowed the 9/11 attacks to be carried out or carried out the attacks themselves.[1]

Other polls show:

• 28% of Americans believe that the Bush Administration is "mostly lying" about what they knew prior to September 11th in regards to possible terrorist attacks against the U.S. [2]

• 49.3% of New York City residents say that the U.S. government "knew in advance that attacks were planned on or around September 11, 2001, and that they consciously failed to act." [3]

Thirty-six percent of Americans equals 108,000,000 people. Millions outside of the U.S. also doubt the official story of 9/11. The evidence reported in the following pages explains why these numbers and percentages are so high.

Controlled Demolition Theory

Belief held by a growing number of individuals for why the World Trade Center Buildings collapsed on September 11, 2001. Nearly one-fifth of Americans now believe that "secretly planted explosives, not burning airplanes" were the cause of the collapse of the Twin Towers collapse.

After extensive research, many scholars have speculated that it would be impossible for an aircraft collision and burning jet fuel to take down a massive steel-enforced skyscraper. These experts believe "controlled explosives" were used to weaken the buildings' foundations, which lead to their collapse.

Most who believe in the "controlled explosion" theory use this evidence to argue that the U.S. government may have had some involvement or prior knowledge of 9/11.

Squibs

Title given to the puffs of smoke that were ejected from lower floors of the Twin Towers just before their collapse.

Many scholars agree that these "squibs" are signs of explosions from within the towers. Many hypothesize that these explosions were thermite incendiary devices that were detonated to help take down the towers.

The presence of thermate (a combination of thermite and other compounds used in incendiary materials) has been found in a molecular analysis of the dust from Ground Zero.

The use of thermite explosives would also explain why molten steel flowed from the tower. It takes around 1500°C to melt structural steel. Hydrocarbon jet fuel burns at a maximium of 825°C. Thermite reactions, on the other hand, occur at 3500°C - 4000°C.

3 Weeks

After 9/11 that pools of molten steel were still under the Ground Zero debris.

The 3500-4000°C temperature of thermite reactions would have provided enough heat to keep the steel in a molten-hot liquid state for this extended period of time. By looking at the fires' colors, most scholars speculate the fires in the WTC towers were between 600-700°C. These fires would not have even melted the steel, let alone kept it in a molten state for several weeks.

Over 50

Documented reports of NY Firemen and rescue team members who heard or saw what seem to be bomb explosions at the North and South Towers.

Here are comments from just a few of them:

"Then a large explosion took place. In my estimation that was the tower coming down, but at that time I did not know what that was. I thought some type of bomb had gone off."

Gregg Hansson -- Lieutenant (F.D.N.Y.)

"It actually gave at a lower floor, not the floor where the plane hit, because we originally had thought there was like an internal detonation explosives because it went in succession: boom, boom, boom, boom, and then the tower came down."

Frank Campagna -- Firefighter (F.D.N.Y.) [Ladder 11]

"It was a frigging noise. At first I thought it was -- do you ever see professional demolition where they set the charges on certain floors and then you hear "Pop, pop, pop, pop, pop"? That's exactly what -- because I thought it was that. When I heard that frigging noise, that's when I saw the building coming down."

Daniel Rivera -- Paramedic (E.M.S.) [Battalion 31]

7 Seconds

Time that it took for World Trade Center Building 7 to collapse. WTC 7 was a 47-story steel-framed skyscraper that was never hit by any plane. However, it fell at 5:20 p.m. on Sept. 11.

The supposed cause of the collapse was uncontrolled fires that were started by burning debris from the North Tower. Many experts report that it would be impossible for fires to cause a free-fall collapse of a skyscraper. Also, video footage before WTC 7's collapse shows no visible evidence of fires within the building.

The building just so happened to house offices for the CIA, FBI, and SEC.

300 feet

Distance WTC 7 stood from the WTC complex. WTC 7 was situated in between the Verizon and Post Office skyscrapers across the street from the North Tower.

The Verizon building actually stood closer to the North Tower, but it only suffered minor damage from falling pieces of debris. The Post Office building was nearly unscathed. Neither the Verizon building, nor the Post Office building caught on fire.

However, WTC7 somehow caught fire, and these fires supposedly brought down this building that housed valuable government information.

3

Steel framed buildings that have collapsed from a fire in all of history. These three are: 1) the North Tower of the WTC, 2) the South Tower of the WTC, and 3) WTC 7.

The only thing that has consistently brought down steel framed buildings in the past is controlled explosives.

Computer hard drives that were recovered from WTC 7 in the Ground Zero cleanup. These computers housed information that proved individuals had profited over $100 million from insider trading during the week of 9/11.

Thousands of other SEC computers were forever lost. These computers housed thousands of sensitive files that dealt with Enron and suspicious stock trades prior to the 9/11 attacks.

No one will ever be able to find the information that the CIA, IRS, SEC, and NSA lost when WTC7 building came crashing down, destroying their computers, files, and records.

$124 Million

Amount of his own money that Larry Silverstein paid to purchase the World Trade Towers six months prior to 9/11. Immediately after the purchase, Silverstein invested in a high-value insurance plan. The buildings were only worth $3.2 billion. He later claimed nearly $5 billion since his insurance plan covered terrorist attacks.

Also, before the events of 9/11, Silverstein expressed interest in tearing down the towers. The large bulky buildings were becoming a huge expense. They had just undergone a $200 million renovation, plus they still needed to remove asbestos. Since a building of that size and location could not be demolished, the building would have to be taken down floor-by-floor. The estimated cost for doing this was $15 billion.

But why pay to dissemble the two towers for $15 billion when you could get a "terrorist attack" to take them down and earn $5 billion in insurance claims?

2,626

Number of lives lost in the 9/11 terrorist attacks. However, Larry Silverstein was not one of them.

Silverstein just so happened to have a doctor's appointment that morning and was not in his office on the 88th floor as usual.

"Pull It"

Phrase spoken by Larry Silverstein about WTC 7. Many believe that this was an order for a controlled demolition of the building.
In a later interview on a PBS documentary, Silverstein spoke these words concerning WTC7:

"We've had such terrible loss of life, maybe the smartest thing to do is pull it. And they made that decision to pull and we watched the building collapse."

8:46 a.m.

Time on 9/11 when the first flight flew into the North building of the WTC.

In a later interview, President Bush said he saw the footage of Flight 11 flying into the North Tower before going into an elementary school classroom. "And I was sitting outside the classroom waiting to go in, and I saw an airplane hit the tower--the TV was obviously on, and I used to fly myself, and I said, 'There's one terrible pilot.'"

However, only one video captured the first plane hitting the North Tower, and it was not shown over TV until September 12th. The second plane had not yet hit the second tower when Bush was outside of the classroom.

Either Bush had access to footage that the rest of the world did not, or he was lying. Most people do not have a hard time believing either is the case.

9:05 a.m.

Time on 9/11 when President Bush was sitting in the classroom in Sarasota, Florida. At this time, the White House chief of staff whispered in his ear, "A second plane has hit the World Trade Center. America is under attack."

Upon hearing the news, Bush sat in his chair showing no expression. The Commander-in-Chief continued to sit in the classroom for another seven to eighteen minutes, reading books with 7-year olds.

We have all been asked, "Where were you on 9/11?" President Bush was reading "My Pet Goat." He found it so interesting that he kept reading it for another 15 minutes before responding to the nation's major crisis.

In a later interview, Bush made the following statement, "Immediately after the first attack I implemented our government's response plans." He did **not** immediately react to the first attack (or the second attack), but he did react rather quickly in declaring war in the Middle East.

6:00 a.m.

Time on 9/11 that a van full of Middle Eastern men pulled up to President Bush's hotel in Sarasota, Florida. The men demanded an interview with Bush but were turned down for not being on his schedule.

Thirty minutes later, Bush took a four-mile jog around the resort with only his secret service guards following.

What is even more interesting is that 9/11 hijackers Mohamed Atta and Marwan Al-Shehhi traveled to Sarasota on September 7, 2001. The two had dinner at a Holiday Inn only two miles from the hotel Bush stayed during his visit to Sarasota on September 10.

John P. O'Neill

Name of a former FBI agent who was an Al-Qaeda expert. In the weeks prior to 9/11, he repeatedly warned the U.S. government of a major terrorist plot.

Due to "conflicts" he was having in the agency, O'Neill was forced to resign from the FBI. Oddly enough, he was immediately reassigned to be the chief of security at the World Trade Center.

He started his new job on September 10, 2001. The next day he was among the 2,626 who died in the WTC buildings. Many believe that O'Neill's death was not a coincidence.

Daniel Lewin

One of the victims killed in Flight 11 that hit the North Tower. However, Lewin was not an ordinary passenger. Lewin was part of the Israeli special forces group Sayeret Matkal.

Sayeret Matkal is an elite and secretive part of the Israeli defense force. Its purpose is to rescue Israeli hostages, gather intelligence, and prevent terrorism. If any one in the world could have stopped the terrorists that day, Lewin would have been that man.

But what's more interesting about Lewin is that he co-founded the Internet company Akamai Technologies. Lewin, a mathematical genius, was able to invent systems that improved the performance of large websites. Among Akamai Technologies' high-profile clients was the U.S. Department of Defense.

Lewin, the computer genius and secretive Israeli intelligence agent, had access to the Department of Defense's website and to computers at the Pentagon. If anyone in the world would have known about America's involvement in 9/11, Lewin would have been that man.

Mahmoud Ahmad

Name of the leader of Pakistani Intelligence during 9/11. During the week prior to 9/11, Ahmad had meetings with both Secretary of State Colin Powell and Director of CIA George Tenet. On the morning of 9/11, Ahmad was having breakfast with Bob Graham, chairman of the Senate Intelligence Committee.

Before his meetings with these major players in the U.S. government, Ahmad had ordered $100,000 to be wired to Mohammed Atta, the "lead hijacker" of the 9/11 terrorist attacks.

Securacom

Name of the security firm for the WTC buildings during 9/11. On Securacom's board of directors is Marvin Bush, the brother of George W. Bush.

Securacom also provided security for Dulles International Airport and United Airlines (two major players in the 9/11 attacks).

Also worth noting: Securacom is financially-backed by Kuwait-American Corp., a company that has had close ties with the Bush family for years. Kuwait-American Corp. is just one of the many connections that the Bush family has with the Middle East and the oil business.

September 10, 2001

Date of the Carlyle Group business conference held in close proximity to the Pentagon. Attendees of the conference include former president George H. W. Bush and Shafig Bin Laden (Osama Bin Laden's brother).

After discussing matters at the conference, Shafig quickly left the country after the September 11th attacks (during a time when all flights were cancelled except for a few special cases).

Also worth noting: the Carlyle Group has large investments in defense companies. Since the start of wars in Iraq and Afghanistan, the Carlyle Group has profited in the billions.

Asia

Destination of the steel from Ground Zero. Immediately after the WTC buildings collapsed, Ground Zero cleanup crews were instructed to ship the 350,000 tons of steel from the site to China and India where it could be recycled.

It is a federal offense to remove evidence from a crime scene. However, the U.S. government had already closed the case 24 hours after the attacks.

By examining the steel from the towers, experts could have determined if demolition devices were used.

Over 1 billion

Number of times the film *Pentagon Strike* has been viewed on the Internet. The six-minute film highlights evidence that no Boeing 757 hit the Pentagon on 9/11.

Millions of forwarded emails and a word-of-mouth Internet marketing campaign caused individuals from all over the world to watch the film on sites like Google Video and YouTube.com. The movie has been translated into 16 different languages and is gaining more total viewers every day.

Zero

Number of videos that show a Boeing 757 flying into the Pentagon. Any of the surveillance cameras on the Pentagon's outer wall could have picked up the event, but none show a plane hitting the Pentagon.

Surveillance cameras from three other sources would have captured the event on tape: 1) the Sheraton Hotel's rooftop surveillance, 2) a gas station's exterior surveillance, and 3) the traffic surveillance of Route 27. All three videos were confiscated by the FBI on the day of 9/11 and have never been released to the public.

Moreover, the Pentagon's interior is under constant video surveillance. Dozens of these videos could have shown a plane barreling through the Pentagon, but none have ever been released.

44 feet 6 inches

Height of the tail of a Boeing 757 airplane. The hole in the Pentagon before it collapsed was about 16 to 20 feet high.

The damage on the Pentagon's facade only extended up to the first two floors of the building (approximately 25 feet from the ground). The height of the airplane's tail would have at least reached the fourth floor.

1 inch

Height above the ground that Flight 77 had to fly to damage the first two floors of the Pentagon. Since the plane's two engines extend five feet below the plane, these engines would have had to been an inch off the ground for the nose of the plane to strike the damage area.

Considering the bulkiness of the commercial airliner, most experts consider this stunt impossible even for the most advanced U.S. Air Force pilot. In actuality, Hani Hanjour piloted the plane.

Six weeks prior to 9/11, an airport in Maryland denied Hanjour the ability to rent a one-man airplane because of his poor flying skills. "He could not fly at all," said a Jet Tech manager, in regards to Hanjour's pilot skills.

Four

Number of cable spools that stood untouched in front of the Pentagon's damage area. These spools were left on the Pentagon's lawn after recent renovations. The largest spool stood over six feet tall and was approximately 25 feet from the Pentagon's outer wall.

Even if Hani Hanjour miraculously maneuvered a Boeing 757 an inch off the ground, it does not explain why these objects in the plane's path remained untouched. This leads many experts to believe something smaller and more nimble than a Boeing 757 hit the Pentagon on 9/11.

63

Out of 64 passengers on Flight 77 that were identified by DNA testing or fingerprinting (the only one not identified was a toddler).

Despite the intense heat generated by 825°C burning jet fuel, officials were able to identify all but one of the victims from Flight 77 that crashed into the Pentagon. However, these same officials were unable to find any pieces of the plane.

There was no trace of the two six-ton plane engines that were made out of nearly-indestructible material, nor any other identifiable part of the plane. The only materials found were small ambiguous pieces that many experts say do not look like parts from a Boeing 757.

According to this evidence, delicate DNA materials withstood the extreme heat and collision, but a highly-advanced aircraft was completely vaporized.

Charles Burlingame

Name of the Naval Reserve Captain who worked as a liaison at the Pentagon for anti-terrorism strategies. Ironically, he was the pilot of Flight 77 that hit the Pentagon on 9/11.

25,000

Approximate number of employees and personnel at the Pentagon on a given day. However, only 125 lives were claimed on 9/11.

The plane hit the only section of the Pentagon that had been renovated for a better defense against a terrorist attack. Since the renovation was still incomplete, most of the impact area was unoccupied by Department of Defense employees. Even though few lives were lost in the Pentagon strike, this section did contain many files that held secret government information, most of which were forever destroyed.

Operation Northwoods

A plan proposed in 1962 by the U.S. Department of Defense and Joint Chiefs of Staff that suggested the U.S would attack itself in order to gain support for military action against Cuba.

This plan called for deaths of American citizens and other acts of terror that would be blamed on the Cuban government. Its purpose was to create a cataclysmic event like a "new Pearl Harbor" that would arouse American willingness for war. Specifically, the plan called for the following acts (see if any sound familiar to 9/11):

• Taking down an unmanned aircraft that would be reported as a commercial aircraft full of innocent passengers.

• Bombing and destroying an American ship harbored at Guantanamo Bay (with real military casualties possibly involved).

• Developing a "Communist Cuban Terror Campaign" in major cities that would be widely publicized by the media.

Luckily, this plan was never implemented. However, it may have been studied by American leaders in the 21st century.

PNAC

Abbreviation for Project of New American Century. PNAC is a neoconservative group established to promote U.S. global leadership. Their pro-war beliefs and foreign relations policies have been heavily criticized for wanting to "take over the world."

When the group was founded in 1997, they hypothesized that several things were needed to ensure U.S. global dominance:

• Significant increase of U.S. military spending;
• Strengthening ties with allies and challenging regimes hostile to US interests;
• Promoting the cause of political and economic freedom outside the U.S.

The group publicly stated that their objectives would not be met without the aid of a "New Pearl Harbor" that would increase military spending and encourage an American willingness for war. Conveniently, 9/11 gave them just what they wanted.

This group is not a group of extremists who keep their identities unknown. Rather, the group is comprised of top members of the Bush Administration. Just to name a few: Dick Cheney (Vice-President), Donald Rumsfeld (former U.S. Secretary of Defense), Paul Wolfowitz (president of the World Bank), Dr. Zalmay Khalilzad (U.S. ambassador to Iraq and Afghanistan), and Jeb Bush (brother of George W. Bush and governor of Florida).

6 weeks

Amount of time that it took the U.S. government to install the PATRIOT Act after 9/11.

The 300-page document was written, passed by both branches of Congress, and signed by the President in a matter of 45 days. In order to prepare this document so quickly, many experts believe that the Bush Administration had started writing it long before 9/11.

$2.5 million

Amount of profits earned by an individual (or organization), who heavily invested in Put Options just before 9/11. Put Options are placed when an investor predicts a stock will fall.

The Put Options were mainly placed on American Airlines and other top corporations that suffered heavy losses due to the 9/11 tragedy.

Never before were so many Put Options of United and American Airlines traded in one day. Normally, Put Options are on a 1:1 ratio with Call Options (investors use Call Options when they predict a stock will increase). On September 7, there was a 12:1 ratio between Put and Call Options.

The most shocking part is that the rightful owner of the $2.5 million still remains unknown.

$46 billion

Current net worth of Warren Buffet, the second richest man in the world.

Around 3:00 pm on 9/11, President Bush arrived at Offutt Air Force Base where he could conduct affairs in a secure location. Oddly enough, Warren Buffet was also at Offutt at that time hosting a golf tournament. The small town of 8,901 just so happened to host the world's most powerful leader and the world's second richest man during one of most crucial dates in U.S. history.

Also worth noting: Buffet's Berkshire Hathaway Co. owns millions of shares of the world's top oil companies.

2nd Largest Oil Reserves

If Warren Buffet is the second richest man in terms of money, Iraq is the second richest nation in terms of oil.

In hopes of gaining more control of oil, the U.S. has long had its eye on grabbing the oil fields in Iraq. Staging a war in Iraq would allow the U.S. to gain Iraqi oil like the Bush family and PNAC have been wanting.

Zero

Number of reprimands in the U.S military for allowing 9/11 to occur. In most societies, top military officials are forced to step down after allowing a major catastrophe. However, after 9/11, most U.S. officials were promoted to higher positions, which were made possible by the increase in U.S. military spending.

It is illogical to think that 19 Muslim terrorists who could barely fly a single-man plane could bypass the most advanced air defense system in the world. U.S. air defense identifies any aircraft that flies off course and dispatches fighter jets to escort these aircraft within minutes. On 9/11, however, they failed to act when three hijacked planes flew off course for over 30 minutes in the two most-protected air spaces on the planet.

11 miles

Distance from Andrews Air Force Base and the Pentagon. Fighter jets could have been scrambled and been at the Pentagon in less than five minutes.

Also, Washington D.C. arguably has the world's most advanced air defense shield protecting its restricted airspace.

$2.3 trillion

Amount of money that was unaccounted for from U.S. military spending on September 10, 2001.

On the day before 9/11, Donald Rumsfeld announced that the Pentagon had lost track of $2.3 trillion worth of transactions. To this day, no one knows what happened to all that money.

To give you a perspective of how much money this is, this is what you could do with $2,300,000,000,000:

•Provide food, clean water, and educational opportunities to 300 million African children for 21 years.[1]
•Purchase a brand new Chevrolet Aveo for everyone in America who is 16 years of age or older.
•Buy **everyone in the world** a mobile phone (which also serves as a digital camera and internet browser), an iPod, a Sony PlayStation 2 (which also serves as a CD and DVD player), a portable television set, and a copy of this book.[2]
•Combine the wealth of Bill Gates, Warren Buffet, and the eight other top 10 richest people in the world, and still be **ten times richer** than the combined wealth of these ten individuals. [3]

Conveniently, the 9/11 terrorist acts made headlines the next day, and this major issue was quickly swept under the rug.

18,500,000

Number of website matches that come up when you search for "The 9/11 Conspiracy Theories" on Google. com. Just to give you a reference, here is what you would get in other Google Searches:

Sexual Intercourse	**1,650,000**
Twin Towers	**1,930,000**
Oprah Winfrey	**2,030,000**
Osama bin Laden	**3,550,000**
The Holy Bible	**6,640,000**
Jesus Christ	**33,200,000**
Democrat	**37,400,000**
George W. Bush	**58,900,000**
Republican	**64,500,000**
Failure	**249,000,000** [1]

[1] Based upon Google search results on December 25, 2006.

To the 2,992 who died on that tragic September day.

Chapter 1

The Pentagon
September 11, 2001
9:40 a.m.

The vacuum from the explosion sucked the oxygen from his lungs as Nathan Alexander crashed to the floor.

The giant explosion devastated Nathan's surroundings. Chairs flipped over, littering the floor with Pentagon employees. Many were hit by collapsing file cabinets. Ceiling tiles rained down.

Nathan quickly jumped up. His pupils dilated as adrenaline rushed through his body. His ears picked up every sound--the cries for help, the groans of pain, the sharp intakes of surprise.

Only moments before, the large corridor that housed the Communications Division had been filled with a click, click, click of keyboards echoing between its marble walls. Now, the sound of tragedy filled the air. Above all the startled voices, a whistling noise grew with staggering intensity. Within seconds, a second blast exploded, leaving a deafening thunder in its wake.

The building rumbled as if it were experiencing an earthquake. Nathan wobbled back and forth as he struggled to keep balance. At 38, the former naval officer was in excellent shape. That, combined with his willpower, helped him stay on his feet while others around him hit the floor.

Although the Pentagon employees were experienced with emergency situations, nothing could simulate the current atmosphere. The piercing alarm and flashing emergency lights added to the commotion.

Fear of the situation caused the military personnel to ignore the protocol of making a calm, orderly evacuation. Within seconds, everyone made a dash to the exit.

Nathan spotted a security officer getting into position at the stairwell for an evacuation. He headed toward him to offer assistance.

"Tell me what to do!" he shouted above the roar.

The security officer motioned toward the door. "Follow everyone else."

Nathan had no intention of jumping ship.

He surveyed the mayhem and spotted several older veterans on the ground, getting trampled by the mad dash to the exit. Thoughts of his wife flooded his mind as he envisioned her experiencing the same destruction and chaos in her office.

Nathan's heart told him to get out as soon as possible, to find Cindy in her section of the Pentagon. His instincts, however, pulled him towards the men on the floor.

He ran to the aid of three fallen figures, helping them to their feet and leading them to the stairwell. Once they were on their way to safety, he'd go for his wife.

Then, it hit him. *My knife.* Nathan turned around and fought through the wave of desperate Pentagon employees.

He got back to his desk and grabbed the knife the President of the United States had awarded to his father for his service as a Navy SEAL. It was more than a memento--his father had earned it by rescuing a band of captured soldiers in Vietnam. It represented who his father was, who Nathan wanted to be. He wanted to hand down this valuable heirloom to his own son. He flashbacked to the moment his father gave him the knife three years ago--it was the day before he died. His father made him promise that he'd always strive to uphold the Alexander family legacy of being true American patriots.

He tucked the knife into his pocket and again sprinted to the exit. He ran into Robert Montgomery, his good friend who frequently collaborated with him on completing the Pentagon's media reports.

Robert began sniffing. "You smell that?"

"Yeah, what is it?" said Nathan, as he nearly tripped by running too fast down the stairs.

"Cordite."

"Cordite? The stuff in explosives?"

"I'd know that smell anywhere--we used it in our artillery shells in the Gulf."

At the base of the stairs, another security officer directed the flow of traffic. Dozens of Pentagon employees struggled to funnel out the exit of the five-story, five-sided building.

Once outside, yet another security officer directed everyone to a vacated parking lot across the street. Nathan broke rank and headed across the lawn, toward the section of the building where his wife worked.

Then he saw it.

A thick cloud of smoke was rising from the west side of the Pentagon. Through the dense black fog, Nathan could see a hole in the face of the building.

His heart sank. *Cindy!*

Chapter 2

Pentagon Lawn
September 11, 2001
9:48 a.m.

Nathan sprinted toward the damaged area.

"Sir!" A security officer stopped Nathan by outstretching his arm. "You can't go any farther."

"My wife's in there!"

"All access to the building is restricted."

"I've got to make sure she's alright." Nathan pushed forward.

The security officer forced his palm into Nathan's chest, preventing him for entering the building. "If your wife's still in there, our people will get her out."

Nathan turned around and sprinted to the parking lot, praying she got out before the fires started. He frantically scanned the tops of the heads of the crowd that had gathered, desperately looking for his wife's golden blonde hair. *Please*, he pleaded silently. *Please.*

His search became increasingly intense with every passing second. He lost all sense of time. He had never known such anxiety-- his heart slammed against his ribs, and his stomach twisted and churned.

As he searched the far side of the lot, a television reporter stuck a microphone in front of his face. Nathan, a communications officer, was accustomed to speaking in front of a camera, but today he had no time for the media.

"Sir, were you in the building when the plane crashed?"

"A plane?" Nathan glanced over the scene. Firefighters were hopelessly battling a ball of fire. "That's what caused this?"

"It's just like what happened in New York earlier today. Were you in the building at the time?"

"Yes."

"Can you tell us about your experience?"

"I didn't know what happened." Nathan was distracted by the flaring flames that engulfed the building. "I'm sorry. I have to find my wife."

As Nathan ran off, an onslaught of security guards reached the news crew. "Pull back!" The guard had his weapon unnecessarily drawn. "That's an order."

"We're civilians. You can't order us—" the newscaster started to say before he was whisked away by the team of security guards.

Nathan waited in parking lot until midnight. The smoldering fires were now extinguished, and all other employees had left. Only dedicated journalists working around the clock to cover the story still lingered. Nathan prayed for a sign that his wife had survived.

He took out his wallet and stared at a family picture. His fingers trembled as he stared into the photo of him standing with Cindy and the kids.

Hearing footsteps, he looked up and saw Robert Montgomery approaching. Nathan had called Robert earlier that afternoon to check on his kids. He now turned to his friend in desperation. "Have you heard anything? How are Nick and Claire?"

Robert slowly kept walking to him, saying nothing.

For several seconds, it felt like time was suspended.

Robert looked into Nathan's eyes. "I'm sorry, Nathan. She didn't make it." Nathan's chin buried into his chest. Robert embraced his friend, letting Nathan's pain run out onto his shoulder.

Chapter 3

The Pentagon
September 13, 2001
7:02 a.m.

Safety crews cleared Nathan's department at the Pentagon at a record pace. His boss, Major Leibner, ordered him to report back to work less than 48 hours after the tragedy.

Leibner walked up to his desk and dropped a six-inch stack of folders in front of him. "Nathan, I'm truly sorry for the loss of your wife. I know you don't want to be here right now, but we have a crisis to take care of. We need you to handle the press releases and the media communications covering the terrorist attacks. These documents have all the facts and descriptions you'll need."

Nathan looked through the list of 19 Middle Eastern names who were the suspected hijackers. "Where did these reports come from?"

"From up top."

"What's the turn-around time on this?"

"ASAP. We'll need you working 24/7 to get this information out. Directive is to structure all reports to awaken patriotic zeal--make every American so proud that they'd be willing to give their life for this country."

Nathan looked at the mug shots of the men who had committed this atrocity. "Done."

Nathan thumbed through the list of 19 hijackers. *How do we already know who did this?*

As he was writing his first report, Nathan felt some of the details regarding the Pentagon attack were not accurate. But he brushed his doubts aside, figuring his emotional state on that day had prevented him from perceiving the events accurately.

One report after another, Nathan handled the Pentagon's media relations regarding the attacks. Meeting deadlines was so demanding that his life was overtaken by his career--he barely had enough time to sleep, let alone to grieve.

Chapter 4

The Pentagon — Office of Special Plans (OSP)
September 8, 2006
11:57 a.m.

Lt. Col. Webber walked into Nathan's private office with a handful of files and papers. "Nathan, I need you to start working on this assignment. The fifth anniversary of 9/11 is Monday, and the media needs an update."

Nathan's face showed his confusion. He was in the Office of Special Plans now. His days of handling media relations were over.

Six months after 9/11, Nathan had asked to be relocated. Writing the reports about the tragedy had simply become too painful. Upper management accepted his request and transferred him to the OSP, a position where he wouldn't have to keep reliving that day over and over.

Webber picked up on Nathan's unspoken question. "You're being assigned to this because we need this report sent out to the media by tomorrow. You wrote most of the official reports after 9/11, so we figured you'd be able to complete this quicker than anyone else in the Communications Division."

"I could probably write it quicker than others, but by tomorrow? Normally an assignment like this takes days."

"Come on, Nathan. You're a Yale grad with a journalism degree--this type of stuff should be easy for you. Make this work for me."

"Maybe if I work nonstop until midnight..." Nathan reluctantly replied.

"That's what I like to hear," said Webber, walking away before Nathan could say anything else.

Nathan let out a long sigh and looked into his computer screen. On his desktop was a family picture taken five years ago. He looked at his teenage daughter Claire. Over the years, she had turned into a beautiful young lady just like her mother had been. Even though she was a mature sixteen-year-old, she'd always be daddy's little girl in his heart. She had recently made her high school's homecoming court and was going to be in her school's football halftime show that night.

He turned his attention to his son, Nick. He could not be prouder of him. He was following in his footsteps by studying at Yale. Nathan wished he could have spent more time with Nick before he left for college, but it seemed that every time they were together it always ended in an argument. Ever since his senior year in high school, Nick insisted there was more to the 9/11 story than Nathan reported. Even though Nathan knew Nick was searching for some kind of tangible justification for losing his mother, he had no patience for conspiracy theories. He also knew believing in such bogus assumptions would cut Nick's chances of going into politics like he wanted his son to do.

His eyes fixated on Cindy. Not a day went by when he did not think of her.

Nathan checked the time: 12:00. He regretted not bringing a lunch. There was no time for a break, but his growling stomach wouldn't leave him in peace until he got something in it.

"That look will put gray hairs on a man's head," said Robert, as he sat down next to Nathan. Even though they no longer worked together in the communications department, Nathan and Robert had remained close friends after 9/11. They usually played tennis together every weekend. Nathan had even made Robert and his wife the godparents of Nick and Claire.

"I'm in a bind. I promised Claire I'd be at her homecoming ceremony tonight, but my boss just gave me a rush assignment that's due tomorrow." Nathan ran his hand through his short brown hair. "I don't know what to do."

"You could use a break," Robert quickly added. "I think you work yourself too hard."

"It has nothing to do working too much. I can—"

Robert interrupted. "Nathan, remember the way you used to work in the Communications Department. You used to kill yourself trying to get all your reports done as soon as possible. Taking some time off once in a while could really help you. That's what I did a few years back--bought a brand new red convertible, maxed-out my vacation time learning how to surf…my wife called it my mid-life crisis. But it was what I needed."

Nathan shook his head. "I don't want material things or a vacation. I just want my life to have more purpose than writing military reports. I'd like to do something that makes an impact on others. I want to wake up in the morning and look forward to life," Nathan paused, then continued with a slight tremble in his voice. "Like I did when Cindy was around."

Nathan returned to his desk and faced the hours of work ahead of him. He looked at Claire's picture on his desktop. *She hasn't had a mother there for her these last five years. I should at least be there for her tonight.*

Nathan was reminded of Robert's suggestion of taking a break. After giving it a quick thought, he opened several documents he had written a few years earlier. He changed the dates and sent them to the media.

Nathan slid out of the office without telling anyone he was leaving. He knew he was asking for trouble, but he wasn't about to let his daughter down.

Chapter 5

Al Tiramisu
September 9, 2006
8:00 p.m.

Nathan had a great weekend. He had stood beside his daughter during her high school's homecoming parade, sharing the special moment with her. All his regrets for taking a shortcut on his reports vanished when she squeezed his hand and thanked him for being there with her.

He had also had a great phone conversation with Nick, despite the fact that Nick had announced he was dropping political science as his major. Nathan had pressured his son to study political science because he wanted him to become a hot-shot politician in Washington--a dream obviously not shared by Nick. The talk reminded him of his own situation 25 years ago when he had to tell his dad that he wanted to study at Yale before joining the Navy. Besides, how could he complain that Nick had decided to follow in his footsteps to become a journalist?

And now he was sitting at one of the finest Italian restaurants in D.C., with his daughter, her friend, and her friend's single mother, Tara. He had easily seen through Claire's transparent efforts to set him up. He'd gone along because it would give him a chance to spend an evening with his daughter and dine at one of his favorite places.

When the girls excused themselves to use the ladies room, Tara slid her chair over so she was directly facing Nathan. "Exactly what is the Office of Special Plans responsible for?"

"We do a little bit of everything, but mainly work with intelligence to plan confidential military affairs."

"Wow. Top secret stuff--sounds interesting."

"My duties aren't as interesting as they sound. I mainly do research and write reports. I also handle a lot of the Pentagon's public relations."

Tara paused briefly to study his face. "Has anyone ever told you that you look like Charlie Sheen?"

Nathan smiled. "Yeah, I've gotten that several times before." He looked over Tara, trying to think of a complimentary line he could say about her in exchange. He examined her blue eyes, but when he did, he saw Cindy's eyes staring back at him. His smile quickly faded.

Tara noticed his obvious reaction, but she tried keeping the conversation going. "You said you were married to someone in the military?"

"I met Cindy right after college. She was already at the Pentagon when I enlisted in the Navy." Nathan kept his response brief; he always felt uncomfortable talking about Cindy.

"My daughter says you were at the Pentagon during the attack. I can't imagine how awful that must have been."

"If you don't mind, I'd rather not talk about it."

Tara moved back noticeably. "I'm sorry."

Nathan slowed his speech, having a hard time getting out something to say. "Yesterday, I had to write a report of what happened five years ago." He sighed. "Anniversaries--they're tough. Once in a while, just for one day, I'd like to forget about it."

Tara leaned forward. "This is probably a stupid question, but have you ever talked to anyone about it? Professionally, I mean." She handed him a business card. "This is a colleague of mine. He specializes in post traumatic syndrome. Many of his clients are military veterans like you."

Nathan studied the card. "So you're a psychologist?"

She laughed lightly. "Guilty as charged. Try as I might, I find myself always studying others' emotions. Forgive me."

"No need to apologize. I appreciate you wanting to help."

From across the room, Nathan saw his daughter weaving her way between tables back to them. She looked so much like his wife. He then looked at his date across the table.

Tara reached out and rested her hand lightly on his. "Are you all right?"

He couldn't do this. He quickly got up from the table, "Please excuse me."

He went directly to the gentlemen's room. He looked in the mirror. Here he was--a military veteran--almost to the point of tears. Tara was right; it was time to stop carrying the past with him.

Chapter 6

Hendricks Counseling Center
September 10, 2006
2:30 p.m.

Nathan lay outstretched on the comfortable leather sofa.

"It's perfectly normal that you still feel grief," said the psychologist, sitting across from Nathan. "Tragically losing a loved one can scar a person for life. In order to overcome your pain, you're going to have to release your emotions--a complete catharsis that sends these negative feelings to the outside. Are you comfortable going back to that day?"

Nathan shrugged. "I suppose."

"Good. Go on."

"I was typing a report, and that's when it happened."

"Don't tell me 'it happened,'" Dr. Lou said. "Describe the situation in detail--describe how the room felt; describe the smell of the air; tell me about the roar of the plane before it crashed into the building."

Nathan thought for a second, then interjected. "But it wasn't a roar--it didn't sound like the thunderous noise that planes make when flying overhead. It was more like a whistle--it was a whistling noise."

"Good, tell me more."

"After the plane crashed, I found myself on the floor. No, wait...I was already on the floor when I heard that whistling noise." Nathan paused briefly, his mind trying to make sense of the events he was describing. "But this doesn't seem right."

"No, keep going," said Dr. Lou. "We sometimes hide things in our subconscious that don't seem right."

Nathan continued to explain his escape, including the confusion that went on. "When I turned and saw the fires, my heart stood still. I had to get to Cindy. But I couldn't go back. The security official wouldn't let me." Nathan stopped for a moment to think. "But how were officials already in place?" he wondered out loud. "It had only been a minute or two after the plane hit."

Before his hour-long session expired, Nathan had gone over the events of the entire day. However, he left the counseling center more confused than ever.

He couldn't get the whistling noise out of his mind. The more he thought about it, the more the sound reminded him of a missile. He had been in the military long enough to know the difference between the sounds of a missile and an airplane. There were several other loose ends that didn't add up. He'd searched everywhere for Cindy. Why hadn't he seen any plane parts? And why were the security guards so adamant about not letting anyone get close the action. He had a lot of questions that needed answers.

As soon as he got home, he got on his computer and did some Googling. He wanted to see if others had heard the same whistling noise he had heard.

He typed "Witnesses at the Pentagon on 9/11" into the search engine. He found pages and pages of links to websites devoted to the subject. Almost every website he visited included testimonies of eyewitnesses who described hearing a "whistling noise." Many of the websites highlighted other discrepancies that occurred at the Pentagon on 9/11--many going to the extent of proposing government conspiracy theories.

Nathan had heard about these crazy "conspiracy theories" before--mainly from his son. He assumed the theories were made up by people who believed in UFOs and still lived in their parents' basements. To his surprise, most of the sites he visited were very professional, providing evidence that they had been prepared by experienced journalists and researchers.

Nathan had spent countless hours writing reports covering what had happened on that day. Reading these new accounts that challenged his prior knowledge of 9/11 was like reading heresy. After some time, however, there was something in him that sided with some of these theories. His brain sided with the Pentagon's official 9/11 report, but his gut insisted that there was more to 9/11 than what he had been told.

What really intrigued Nathan about these stories was the fact that there was nothing on the Internet--no Web site, no personal Web page, no news footage--that showed any clear airplane parts from the Pentagon's wreckage. Some websites showed pieces of debris and claimed that they were aircraft parts, but these pieces were so obscure that they could have been anything.

He thought back five years ago, trying to remember seeing an airplane. But he couldn't. There was fire, and lots of smoke; but he never saw any parts of a plane. He was right on top of the action when the security guard prevented him from going inside. Yet he did not recollect seeing any skid marks or airplane wreckage.

He surfed the Internet for another four hours that night, riding the "9/11 Conspiracy" wave for hours. It was amazing how much evidence people had compiled that supported these conspiracy theories.

The last website he visited begged the question that ran through every site: was September 11th an inside job?

Nathan tossed and turned in his bed, tormented by thoughts that wouldn't let him rest: *is there more to 9/11 than I've been told? Have all my reports been based on partial truths?* Certainly all his sources were undeniable facts--they had all came from the top military and government officials. *Why would anyone in our own government want to lie about this?*

Before he fell asleep, he convinced himself that the 9/11 Conspiracy Theories were just that--*theories*. There were rational explanations that could counter every theory he had read. There was no reason that these websites should conflict with the information that was coming from the most powerful institution in the world.

Chapter 7

The Pentagon
September 11, 2006
6:55 a.m.

Walking into work, Nathan passed protestors holding signs and shouting grievances. He'd gotten used to it. Every day a new group met outside the Pentagon to protest the Iraq war or U.S. military actions. He had learned the best way to deal with it was to walk fast without making eye contact.

As he neared the entrance to the Pentagon, something made him stop. One of the protestor's signs read, "9/11 was an INSIDE JOB."

Behind the shouting protestors was a table the group had set up to distribute information. Out of curiosity, Nathan approached the gray-haired man tending the table.

"What's all this about?" Nathan asked.

"We're handing out information that tells people the truth about 9/11. This being the fifth anniversary of the attacks, we figured it would be an appropriate time to educate people on what really happened."

Nathan picked up one of the pamphlets. "There seems to be a lot of people that believe these alternate stories."

"Yes. Millions around the world are a part of the Truth Movement."

"Truth Movement?"

"That's what we call ourselves--those of us who believe that the 'official' 9/11 story isn't completely true. But there's a wide range of beliefs in the Movement." The man pointed to the young protestors to his left as he continued. "Some of us, like those college students, believe in theories that say the government orchestrated the attacks. They obviously use their youthful energy to voice their opinion. I, on the other hand, believe the government had prior knowledge of al-Qaeda's attacks, and they let them happen so they could lead this country to war."

"How did you come to this conviction?" Nathan asked.

"I'm a history professor at Georgetown. My colleagues at the university showed me scientific research and solid evidence that proved 9/11 goes beyond what the media has reported."

The professor nodded toward Nathan's hand. "That pamphlet you're holding has a list of websites that opened up my eyes." He reached for a book under the table and handed it to Nathan. "Here, why don't you take this? It's a great book on the subject."

Nathan read the title: *The New Pearl Harbor*. He glanced at his watch. "I need to get to work, but thank you for the material."

"You work at the Pentagon?"

"Hopefully. I left Friday on a bad note. With any luck, I'll still have a job."

Nathan entered his office and signed onto his computer. As expected, he had an email from a superior who greatly disapproved of his tactic of changing the dates and distributing an old report. Nathan could feel the anger emitting from the screen. He immediately replied with an email back, committing to working 12 hours a day to get the reports completed properly.

Later, as he ate a sandwich he'd brought to work, he took out the pamphlet the professor had given him and started visiting the websites it referenced. In the span of his lunch hour, he traveled through a myriad of websites covering the hidden truths behind 9/11. He discovered that the 9/11 conspiracy theories went beyond the discrepancies concerning the Pentagon. There was even more questionable evidence concerning the collapse of the World Trade Center buildings.

As he wrote the government report concerning 9/11 that afternoon, Nathan was hesitant in including the details of the official 9/11 story. Now that he had seen things from a different perspective, he had a hard time trying to clear these thoughts from his mind.

Later that evening, after everyone had left the OSP sector, Nathan again accessed the Internet to do some research about 9/11. He wanted to know more, and he wanted to know the truth.

Chapter 8

The Pentagon
September 12, 2006
9:12 p.m.

Nathan walked back to his car after his second consecutive 12-hour workday. Even though he nearly spent the entire day on the computer, he was eager to go home and get on the Internet. At the same time, he scoffed at himself for his fascination with what he had always considered "outrageous conspiracy theories."

He continued walking, so engrossed in his thoughts that he failed to sense a person crouching in a small patch of shadows. As he walked past the shadows, the hooded figure quickly reached out and grabbed Nathan by his shoulders. Nathan gasped as his upper body was jerked back. Instinctively, he broke free of the stranger's grip and pushed the figure away from him. His eyes immediately scanned the assailant's body for any sign of a gun, knife, or other weapon.

The hooded figure quickly stepped back into shadows, staying a good distance back from Nathan. "Relax, I don't want your wallet. I just need to know your motives."

Nathan held his hands in tight fists, instinctively posed and ready to defend himself. "Motives? What are you talking about?"

"You visited several objectionable websites from your office--sites that debase government authority. Who gave you the orders to visit these sites?"

"I'm a writer. I do research," he said, trying to shown no sign of alarm.

"And what have you concluded?" the assailant asked, sounding somewhat irritated.

"I don't know. I was just curious."

The unknown figure inched forward and handed Nathan a folded piece of paper. "If you want to know the truth, meet me at this time tomorrow night at this location. Come alone."

The figure walked off, disappearing into the darkness.

Nathan stood motionless. Had he just met a friend or foe?

Chapter 9

The Pentagon
September 13, 2006
8:40 p.m.

Nathan looked at the address on the paper: *1227 Ridgeway Ave.* He had already checked Google Maps, and it had nothing listed at this location.

What have I gotten myself into? Could this unknown figure be U.S. Intelligence, questioning if I'm anti-government? What if this person actually knows secret information about 9/11? But who'd know what websites I visited except for top Pentagon authorities?

For over an hour, Nathan wondered what he should do. Finally, he looked down at his father's knife on his desk. Its inscription read: "Truth, Honor, and Justice."

Truth, he whispered to himself, thinking of what his father would do in the situation.

Without hesitation, Nathan grabbed the slip of paper with the address and walked out with the knife tucked securely in his pocket.

His search brought him to a part of town that he was unfamiliar with. As he approached a dark alley in front of him, his mind raced with apprehension and doubt. *I can't believe I'm doing this.*

Nathan paused briefly to let his eyes adjust to the dark. The only source of light in the alley came from a small hotel on the corner. Nathan tried to keep quiet, but his footsteps echoed throughout the desolate passage. His sweaty palm had a death-grip around the knife in his pocket.

He eventually came across a metal door to a large brick building. Just enough light from the hotel escaped down the alley for Nathan to see *1227* written on the outside. Nathan took a deep breath and reached for the door knob. He pulled slowly--the screeching sound of rusty hinges echoed throughout the narrow alley. His heart raced, knowing that his entrance was anything but secret.

Darkness filled the room when the door closed behind him. Nathan extended his arm but was unable to see his hand.

"Hello?"

"Mr. Alexander, I'm glad you've come," said the same voice from the night before.

Nathan could sense the presence of the figure to his right but was unable to get a look at him. "Who are you?"

"Someone who has spent the last five years hiding because of what I know about 9/11."

"And who do you think I am?" Nathan demanded.

"I know you're the son of a distinguished Navy SEAL who also has spent time in the Navy. You worked in the Communications Department at the Pentagon handling public relations until you were relocated a few years back. You also had a wife who was murdered on 9/11."

Nathan's attention snapped to a new level upon hearing the mentioning of his wife. "How do you know this? Are you with the government?"

"I've never been involved with the U.S. government. And how I'm able to get my information is irrelevant at this time." The figure took a step closer to Nathan. "Before we proceed, I need to know if you will help me."

"I don't even know who you are or what you want, yet you want me to commit to helping you?"

"Need proof that you can trust me? That's reasonable enough." The figure moved toward Nathan in a non-threatening manner and extended a piece of paper. "Here..."

"What's this?"

"Open your cell phone and read it yourself."

Nathan opened his cell phone and used its light to view the paper. He immediately recognized the first line. "Where did you get this?"

"Let's just say I'm good at retrieving information from computers."

"But this is from an email account nobody's used in years."

"That's right--not since your wife died. In fact, that's the last email she sent. As you'll read--she, too, had questions about the truth."

"And she knew you? She sent this to you?"

"I never had the honor of meeting your wife, and she certainly didn't intend that email for me. But this proves that she had questions about events that were going on shortly before her death. I'm offering you a chance to pick up where she was forced to leave off."

The hooded figure gave Nathan a moment to absorb the information. "Why didn't she tell me?" he finally asked.

"Would you have listened? A lot of people are too naive to accept the fact that their own government is involved in corrupt activities. But she also knew she'd be endangering your life by entrusting you with this information."

Nathan's body tensed. "What do you want from me?"

"I've come upon a critical point in my research. I've almost got all I need to expose the truth behind the September 11th attacks. But I need several pieces of evidence that I don't have access to--evidence only someone within the Pentagon could get."

"You want me to steal classified government information?" asked Nathan, shocked at the audacity of this stranger.

"I will not lie to you, Mr. Alexander. You will be risking your life. But what you'll find could dramatically change the future. And, even to a small degree, avenge your wife's untimely death."

Nathan thought for several seconds. "What do you want me to do?"

"Before we discuss this, it's important that you know the proper security measures that will prevent you from being caught. Take this piece of paper." Nathan felt the man slide another piece of paper into his palm. "It has access information to a secure email address. We will use this as our predominant form of communication."

"What's so special about this email address?"

"It's completely untraceable. The U.S. government has access to every email that is sent. A filter catches key words like 'bombs,' 'terrorist attack,' or '9/11 conspiracy' and sends red flags to U.S. intelligence forces. Even if one of our communications is flagged, no one could ever trace it back to your computer."

"So I could write emails from the Pentagon, and they could never trace it back to me?"

"Exactly. Tomorrow I'll send you instructions on what I need via email." The figure backed toward the corner. "That's all I needed from you tonight. I hope you'll go home now and consider helping me in this pursuit."

Nathan turned to the door, but was stopped by the figure's voice. "And another thing, Mr. Alexander. I suggest you don't look at any websites concerning the 9/11 Truth Movement while you're at work. You'll be safe viewing them from your home, but there's always a set of eyes watching you at the Pentagon."

Nick Shelton

Chapter 10

The Pentagon
September 14, 2006
7:05 a.m.

Nathan sat down at his desk and unfolded the piece of paper.

This is your email access. Shred this as soon as you have read and memorized it.

Address: www.boc.ix
Username: T.Ruth
Password: 911Truth

Nathan opened his Internet browser and entered the unusual web address. He looked over his computer to make sure no one was coming his way. Now that he was in the OSP, he had his own office. However, with an open door policy, his superiors were constantly stepping in.

The website looked like a typical email login page. He entered his username and eight-digit password. He pressed *Enter* and saw he had one email in his mailbox:

Subject: 1ˢᵗ Assignment
From: DL@boc.ix
To: T.Ruth@boc.ix
Date: 9/13/06

T.Ruth,

I am grateful you have decided to pursue this endeavor with me. I hope we will remain focused on uncovering the truth.

Your first assignment:
I need the complete list of passengers for Flight 11 that flew into the North WTC Tower. Specifically, I want the 19 names that appear on the official flight manifest – not the names from the government's list of passengers that has been previously released.

As you know, you can only access this information from a computer in the Communications Dept. Since you used to work at this dept, I'm sure you can find a way to access their network and look for the transcripts that date back to September 11ᵗʰ and 12ᵗʰ of 2001.

If you're successful in finding this information, please report back to me tonight – same time and place.

Sincerely,
D L

Nathan leaned back in his chair and considered the risk involved. He hit the reply button and typed the following:

This would require me to hack into government information. If I get caught, I'd not only be fired, but I'd have to serve jail time. I just don't know if I can trust you.

As soon as he finished typing his reply, he got an idea for an easy way to get this information. His plan was relatively safe, but the consequences were enormous.

For the next several hours, he debated what he should do. He kept telling himself that the stories that countered the official 9/11 report were nonsense. *Can I really risk my future on what could be a hoax?*

Nathan then thought about what the figure said about his wife. Something in him told him that he needed to get to the bottom of this. One look into his desktop's picture of their family portrait convinced him it was worth the risk.

Just before noon, Nathan walked through the Pentagon's maze of hallways and sectors to the Communications Department. He knocked on Robert's office door.

"Hey, Nathan. I was just about to go to the cafeteria to see if you were there."

"I'm actually going to skip lunch today. I really need to finish those reports about the 9/11 anniversaries."

"The ones that were due Friday?"

"Yeah, it's a long story, but I didn't get them done in time. Anyway, I need access to some of the 9/11 documents. Since I'm in hot waters with Lt. Col. Webber, could I get them off your computer, instead of having to ask him for them?"

"Sure, go ahead. You want me to bring you back anything from the cafeteria?"

"Yeah, some fruit or anything healthy would be great."

As soon as Robert left, Nathan scampered back to Robert's computer. He moved the mouse before the password-protection screen appeared. All Pentagon computers had a three-minute delay--if the computer sat idle for longer than three minutes, a screen appeared which prevented anyone else from logging on to it.

Nathan accessed the Communication Department's Intranet network. He searched through the September 11th documents.

Despite his hurried efforts, he was unable to quickly find what he was looking for.

Finally, he found a document with a list taken from the official flight manifest. He scrolled down the screen, looking for the Middle Eastern names. However, he did not find any. He went back to the top and tried looking again, this time scrolling down slower. But as he did so, Robert came walking through the door, holding an apple in his hand.

"Still looking through the stuff?"

Nathan instinctively closed all the screens on the computer. "I was just finishing up. I think I got what I need." As a researcher and journalist, Nathan tried not to make a habit of lying. However, his work with communicating government information had taught that sometimes it was necessary to leave out certain details.

Nathan walked out of the office disappointed at not finding what he was looking for.

That night at his home, Nathan researched more about Flight 11. From his personal computer, he was able to find pictures and biographies of all the passengers on the flight. However, he was unable to find the official flight manifest.

Nathan walked down the dark alleyway. This time he was smart enough to bring a flashlight. Before entering, he examined the building from the outside. It was an old brick building that was undoubtedly an abandoned warehouse.

He entered the door and pointed his flashlight in all directions, exploring the darkness surrounding him.

"Are you there?" he asked.

From his left, the figure swooped in and yanked the flashlight from Nathan's hands. He turned it off and moved a good distance away. "I'd like to keep my identity unknown until I can trust you."

"Trust me? I'm the one who's risking my life and career for someone I don't even know."

"Did you do homework like I asked?"

"I got into the Communication Department's network, and was even able to pull up a document that had a list of names from the flight manifest--but I never found the nineteen hijackers' names. I found several websites that had the pictures and information of all the passengers on the flight, but not the official American Airlines list from that day."

"So you read about the Flight 11 passengers on the list?"

"All 92 of them."

The figure took a few steps to the corner. He flipped a switch and several lights illuminated the corner of the abandoned warehouse.

Nathan stared into the face of this man. He thought he was seeing a ghost.

Chapter 11

1227 Ridgeway Ave.
September 14, 2006
9:11 p.m.

Nathan studied the man's face. "You're--you're one of the guys from the list. Lewin--the one who was shot by one of the hijackers."

A hint of a smile widened across the man's ruddy face. "That's right. Daniel Lewin." He extended his hand. "My death is another lie in the 9/11 story."

"Your picture and bio were at the top of the list," Nathan shook Lewin's hand energetically. "The website said you were the first victim of the 9/11 attacks. You were shot before the hijackers took over the cockpit."

"Shot with a gun the hijackers didn't have," said the 36-year-old Lewin, lowering the hood of his sweatshirt. "If you remember the official report correctly, the hijackers took over the plane with box cutters and knives. They never had guns."

"But how did you survive?"

"I wasn't on the plane. I boarded it, but as I was taking my seat, an inside source called and ordered me to get off the plane. I was able to quietly exit before they closed the door to the terminal."

"The inside source--the website said you were a part of the Israeli special forces. Secret Markal, if I'm not mistaken."

"That's *Sayeret Matkal*," said Daniel in a polished Israeli accent. "And yes, I was a part of that organization."

"I didn't read much about it, but it's like a group of secret agents, right?"

"A group of Israeli James Bonds, if you will. But it's not like members of Sayeret Markal are constantly on top-secret missions for the Israeli government. We have normal roles in society. We're just expected to help Israel in times of crisis or terrorism."

Nathan looked down, trying to think back to the website. "You're a mathematician, right? That co-founded an Internet company?"

"Yes, a multibillion-dollar corporation to be exact."

"Multi-billion?"

"Akamai was providing web solutions to the top organizations in the world-- including the U.S. Army, Navy, Air Force, and other Department of Defense branches at the Pentagon."

Nathan was astonished. "Akamai builds websites for the DoD?"

"No, Akamai doesn't build websites. We improve the performance of current websites and networks. What do you know about Internet caching?"

"Not much."

"Basically, when you visit a website, your computer retrieves all that information from another computer--for example, the Pentagon's mainframe. But instead of having to retrieve information from the Pentagon's server every time you access a DoD website, the information is compressed and saved in a specific folder, or 'cache,' so your computer doesn't have to download everything again. You following so far?"

Nathan nodded.

"At Akamai, we have thousands of servers set up around the world that hold these cache files for our clients."

"So, basically Akamai holds these compressed files of information for government agencies."

"Precisely. Compressed files that I have access to. And we're not just talking about websites. We're talking about the intranet networks also, the agencies' internal sites. Thus allowing me to see what's going on at the Pentagon and countless other places."

"Hold on. If you have access to the Pentagon's network, why did you need me to find the information about the Flight 11's flight lists?"

"I didn't--I've known that information for years. I just wanted to see if you could find it."

"I could've been arrested!" Nathan's voice echoed throughout the large warehouse. "I did it for no reason?"

"Consider it practice," replied Daniel nonchalantly. "And I'd hoped you'd be curious enough to dig deeper, which would give you a chance to learn a little bit about me."

Nathan did not know if he was standing in front of a mastermind genius or an imposter who was working for the government. Either way, he had inside information on the events of 9/11. "So what else do you know about 9/11?"

"You might want to sit down for this."

Chapter 12

1227 Ridgeway Ave.
September 14, 2006
9:20 p.m.

Daniel eased onto the concrete floor. "Make yourself comfortable," he said, patting the floor next to him.

Nathan squatted beside him, noticing that the floor and walls were covered in symbols written in chalk. The sight reminded him of several movies he had seen that depicted professors and scientists who wrote their theories and equations on walls and windows. "What's all this?"

"Some of my research--I like giving myself a visual for the connections of events and people involved. I write everything in Hebrew in case anyone happens to stumble across this place."

Nathan looked around the warehouse. The room wasn't much larger than a standard-size high school gym. Other than a few wooden crates scattered haphazardly across the floor, the warehouse was empty. "Is this where you live?"

"No, I stay in the hotel on the corner."

"How do you pull that off? Have you created a new identity?"

"No. I'm able to hack into the hotel's computer from my laptop. I look for what rooms are vacant on a given night, and I take my pick. I stole one of the maid's keycards, so I have access to all the rooms."

Nathan laughed. "Sounds like you are one smart guy."

Daniel kept a serious tone without cracking a smile. "I don't want to sound arrogant, but, yes, I do have a high IQ and exceptional computer skills. But it hasn't been my brain that's gotten me this far--it's been sheer determination to uncover the truth."

As Nathan's eyes adjusted to the darkness, he made out a stack of bottled water and food wrappers in a nearby corner. "How long have you lived like this?"

"Here in D.C.? Only a few months. After 9/11, I stayed in Boston with some friends I could trust. I was able to get some cash to live on, but nothing compared to the millions I had in Akamai stock."

"So you went from living in a mansion to stealing a night's stay in hotel rooms?"

Daniel waved his hand, dismissing the inconvenience. "Mere creature comforts. The toughest part of living in secrecy has been not being able to see my family." Daniel rose, gesturing for Nathan to follow.

He led the way to a stack of notebooks and a laptop computer hidden under a crate in a corner. "My research keeps me busy--I don't have much time to dwell on the past."

Nathan's eyes looked up and down the towers of notebooks and files. "All this is 9/11 research?"

"It may look like a lot, but it's all I have to show for the last five years. After staying in Boston a couple of years, I traveled to New York City and compiled a lot of research on the Twin Towers. I'm now here in Washington to get what I need from the Pentagon."

"Which is?"

Daniel took a deep breath. "First, let me briefly tell you what I know about 9/11."

They took a seat on crates, which were only slightly more comfortable than the cold concrete floor. Nathan crossed his legs and leaned forward, hungry now for all the information he could get.

"There are several reasons why 9/11 occurred--four major ones by my count. Number one is political agendas of certain politicians. Number two deals with oil and energy. Number three deals with the American economy and certain corporations that benefited from the catastrophe. And the fourth has to do with top secret information held at the Pentagon."

Nathan tried to make sense of the four reasons, but words like al-Qaeda, Afghanistan, and bin Laden were echoing in his head. "You said something about politicians--you mean politicians in American or in the Middle East?"

"I'm talking about President Bush and his cabinet members. A select group of them planned the 9/11 attacks. Many of these high-ranking officials also had a hand in Numbers 2, 3, and 4. You'll need to do some research before you can understand the complex web these radical conservatives constructed out of 9/11. I'll send you an email later tonight that'll get you started."

"I'll look into it." Nathan said skeptically. Nathan was not loyal to one political party, but he was suspicious at how Daniel immediately pointed out that 'conservatives' were the ones involved. Instead of questioning Daniel's political views, he tried continuing the conversation. "You talked about oil and energy--I can see your point on how it's a central motive. All the OSP's reports concerning the War in Iraq are about oil. It's basically what the war in the Middle East boils down to."

"I'm sure your knowledge of the Pentagon's strategy for Iraq will help me with my research. But there's a lot more under the surface of the 'Oil War.' We'll get to that later. There's also a lot going on behind the scenes with the American corporations involved in 9/11. Numbers 2 and 3 are linked in many ways."

"You mentioned 'Top Secret Information at the Pentagon.' What do you mean by that?"

"I'm not exactly sure of what it entails. But whatever it is, the government has shown a great interest in it, and they're making sure the rest of the world never finds out about it. It's why I'm here in Washington."

Nathan thought to himself for some time, trying to make sense of what he was being told. "I just don't know if I can believe this. Our own government behind an attack on U.S. citizens?"

"Start your research. Look into the motives of the neoconservative political groups before you start making judgments."

"It's not just about the corrupt politicians. It's this whole notion that our government could do such a hideous act."

"What's the alternative?" Daniel demanded. "That 19 men hijacked four planes with box cutters, infiltrated the most advanced air defense system in the world, piloted commercial aircrafts even though they couldn't fly a single-propeller plane, and managed to defy the laws of gravity by taking down two 110-story building in perfect symmetrical fashion?"

Daniel walked over to get a manila folder from his large stack of files. "Maybe this will help." He took an 8½ x 11 photo out of the folder and handed it Nathan. "What do you see here?"

Nathan studied the black and white picture. It looked like an aerial photo of an airplane sitting in a hangar. "It looks like a small private jet. But, no, it can't be--it's wings are too narrow and it's fuselage is too small to be a passenger jet. What is this?"

"It's called a Global Hawk aerial vehicle. Global Hawks are unmanned aircraft with highly sophisticated GPS navigation systems. Someone in New York City could pinpoint that thing to hit an archer's bulls-eye in Los Angeles. They're normally used for reconnaissance missions, but on 9/11, I believe it was used as a missile."

Nathan glanced up from the picture with a skeptic look. "You think this hit the Pentagon?"

"You tell me. You're the one that was there that morning. All I know is that there's no video footage showing a commercial airliner crashing into the Pentagon."

Nathan studied the picture again. He now spoke in a curious tone. "Would one of these make a whistling noise?"

"Traveling at 400-500 mph—it'd make a high-pitched whistling noise. Quite different than a commercial aircraft. I'm guessing this is what you heard from your office?"

Nathan nodded, unable to speak.

"Mr. Alexander, can I trust that you'll help me find who is responsible for sending this into the Pentagon?"

Nathan took another long look at the picture. Memories of Cindy flooded his head. "Count me in."

Chapter 13

3211 Fourth Street NE
September 14, 2006
11:55 p.m.

As soon as he got home, Nathan wasted no time to check his email. Sure enough, a new message awaited him.

Subject: The Political Agendas of 9/11
From: DL@boc.ix
To: T.Ruth@boc.ix
Date: 9/13/06

T.Ruth,

Look these up:
•Search Wikipedia.org for "PNAC"
These are major contributors to 9/11. They had the power and knowledge to plan the attacks.

•Google: Operation Northwoods
See if you can find the connection between this military plan and 9/11.

•Search Wikipedia for "One World Government"
See if you find any connections with the other two.

This will give you some background on the neocon agenda and one of the main reasons for 9/11.

Sincerely, D L

Nathan started with *PNAC*. He skimmed through an encyclopedia article entitled
"Project of the New American Century." He discovered PNAC was a group of "neoconservatives" whose purpose was to plan American global domination. His eyes came to a halt when he read the names of members of this political organization. *Paul Wolfiwitz, Dick Cheney, Jeb Bush...*

He immediately sent Daniel an email.

DL,
We need to talk. I need to tell you what I know about one of the PNAC members.
Sincerely,
T.Ruth

Daniel's story was suddenly becoming much more believable.

Chapter 14

3211 Fourth Street NE
September 15, 2006
5:35 a.m.

Nathan woke up before the sun, eager to continue his Internet research.

Nathan started researching where he left off the night before by digging deeper into PNAC. He could not believe there was a formal organization whose purpose was to ensure that America would turn into the greatest superpower in world's history. Worse, this organization appeared to be comprised of the nation's top military and political leaders.

Nathan visited Internet forums where hundreds of Americans expressed their concerns for PNAC's goals. Almost all acknowledged PNAC as a group of power-hungry individuals who'd go to any measure to try to take over the world.

Most believed PNAC's goals would cause the downfall of the United States. Since its creation in 1997, PNAC had desperately wanted to gain control of Iraq. It wasn't a stretch for Nathan to believe this--working in the Office of Special Plans, he already knew the War on Terrorism had little to do with terrorism. It was more about oil, power, and money.

After reading the information about PNAC, Nathan Googled "Operation Northwoods." He learned it was a government plan the Pentagon had submitted to President John F. Kennedy in 1962. It called for the United States to orchestrate a fake terrorist attack against itself to start a war against Cuba. *If top*

Pentagon officials planned to kill their own citizens in the 60s, what's stopping them from doing the same thing 50 years later? Politicians and military officials certainly haven't become more moral or ethical.

This fake terrorist plan was designed to recreate a "new Pearl Harbor." Nathan remembered reading this line the night before. He Googled *PNAC* again. There it was: in September 2000, top PNAC members wrote a report that stated a "new Pearl Harbor" was needed to accomplish their goals. *PNAC used the exact same words to script their fake terrorist plot.*

Nathan searched through his briefcase for the book the professor had given him in front of the Pentagon. He grabbed it and turned it face up--*The New Pearl Harbor.*

A wave of nausea hit him. Something wicked, unthinkable, unimaginable was going on within the highest level of the U.S. government.

Nathan returned to *Wikipedia* and typed "One World Government." Immediately, a page entitled "The New World Order" filled his screen. He scanned the information and quickly learned that the NWO is a theory proposing that the world's developing society is growing toward a unified world government. The theory suggests that key figures from international government, banking, commerce, and mass media will be involved.

Nathan quickly referenced PNAC's membership list and examined the occupations of its members. Their titles included:

- the second-highest political figure in the U.S. government – Dick Cheney,
- the president of the World Bank – Paul Wolfowitz,
- the head of the Department of Defense – Donald Rumsfeld
- the U.S. ambassador of Afghanistan and Iraq - Zalmay Khalilzad,
- the director for the International Broadcasting Bureau

- Seth Cropsey
- U.S. representatives for NATO and the U.N.
- top members of the Department of State
- and world-renowned professors from Harvard and Yale.

And that list was just the beginning--dozens of other PNAC members held prestigious occupations in Washington and in foreign relations. PNAC certainly had plenty of key figures from international government, banking, commerce, and mass media.

Nathan stared at the computer screen in disbelief. *Can this be? Are the politicians in PNAC trying to start a New World Order. Or worse, did the NWO create PNAC to carry out its plan of achieving a unified global government?*

Before going off to work, he wanted to see what else he could find out about Daniel. He typed "Daniel Lewin" into Google, and the search warranted hundreds of results, many of them displaying Daniel's picture.

Nathan looked through the pictures of Daniel taken before 9/11--there was no doubt that the man from the warehouse was the same man. It looked like he had lost a good amount of weight over the last five years. It also looked like his skin complexion was now a little lighter, probably the result of not spending much time in the sun. But even in the photographs taken before 9/11, Daniel had a fairly light complexion--his skin color looked more like a white American male rather than a man from Israel.

At work, Nathan finished the 9/11 press reports. After emailing them to the list of media outlets, he considered the irony of sending information that he was now beginning to doubt.

After emailing and faxing all the reports, he decided to call a reporter he knew on the professional and personal levels.

"Hello, Gary Smith, *Time Magazine*," answered the voice on the other end of the line.

"Gary, Nathan Alexander from the Pentagon's Office of Special Plans. I just emailed you a report on 9/11 that you requested."

"Great."

"Sorry I didn't get it to you sooner, but I needed time to reflect this past week. This time of the year always brings up tough memories."

"No problem."

"I'm also calling because I have a question for you about 9/11."

"Shoot."

"Are you familiar with the 9/11 conspiracy theories that have millions of followers on the Internet?"

"I'd be a pretty poor reporter if I didn't. Have to keep a pulse on the masses--crazy ideas or not." He hesitated briefly and added tentatively, "You know, some of them actually have some good points."

"I agree. So tell me--why haven't you, not you personally, but you as the mainstream media, not reported these views?"

"Are you kidding? It'd be journalistic suicide."

"How so?"

"First off, my editor would never approve of something that would hint of government wrongdoing on such a scale. And if it somehow did get printed, I'd be branded as anti-government--and that'd be the end of my career as a journalist."

"What makes you think your editor would never approve it? We're talking the story of the century."

"Business. Money. It always comes down to those two things. My editor has to report to the corporate executives. And the corporate execs would never print anything that's associated with being anti-American or anti-American."

"But what if some of these things are true?"

"It wouldn't matter. The corporate execs only care about making money. To make money you have to have Uncle Sam and corporate America on your side. So as long as they're running stories that the government wants, these execs rake in billions."

"Billions? From *Time* magazine?"

"Not *Time*. I'm talking about the execs of AOL Time Warner, the company that owns *Time*." Gary took a breath and started talking faster, his tone increasingly angry. "They own AOL, CNN, *Sports Illustrated*, Warner Bros., *People* magazine, *DC Comics*--and dozens of other huge media outlets."

"Sounds like they have a monopoly of the media."

"You got that right. And it's not just Time Warner. Four other conglomerates are a part of the 'Big Five' that own American media. They own all the mainstream magazines, television channels, radio stations, book publishers, and Hollywood studios." Gary took another breath to calm down. "Sorry for going off on a rant. As you can tell, this is an issue I'm concerned about."

"No. Thanks for telling me this--I think this is something that every American should know." Nathan looked down at the time. "I need to be going now. Have a good day, Gary."

"You too, Nathan."

Nathan leaned back in his chair and thought about what Gary had just told him. Nathan remembered several instances when the Pentagon forced the media to run specific stories. In certain situations, Nathan was told to "bully" any journalists who were unwilling to run stories the Pentagon wanted. What he did not know was the extent the government's influence had over the media executives as to what the American people could and could not hear.

No wonder these stories on 9/11 have been kept a secret.

Chapter 15

1227 Ridgeway Ave.
September 15, 2006
8:55 p.m.

Nathan opened the warehouse door and found a dim light illuminating the corner. Under it, Daniel was writing in a notebook.

Daniel put down his pen to acknowledge his guest. "Mr. Alexander–"

"Please, call me Nathan," he interrupted.

"Sure thing, Nathan. So what did you think of the information on PNAC?"

"I couldn't believe it." Nathan walked to Daniel's location in the corner. "I've never heard of them before, but it sounds like they're running this country."

"And they'll be running this world if we don't do something."

"I know. They're the prefect description of the One World Government or New World Order--whatever you call it. And Operation Northwoods--the PNAC guys basically used it as a rough draft for 9/11."

"Good way to put it." Daniel flipped back several pages in his notebook. "Listen to this--I just discovered this today. You read about the Pentagon presenting the Northwoods Plans to President Kennedy, right?"

"Yes, in 1962. Right before Kennedy was assassinated."

"And you remember how the PNAC members call themselves neoconservatives?"

"Yeah, that's what they call their radical conservative beliefs."

"Well, the neoconservative movement emerged into American politics during the Kennedy administration--which means there were a good many neoconservatives in the Kennedy administration who were very familiar with Operation Northwoods. After this first generation of neocons retired from office, they became professors at Ivy League schools-- namely Harvard and Yale. At these schools, they taught their neoconservative beliefs to the 20-year-old students who are now a part of..."

"PNAC," Nathan said, finishing Daniel's sentence.

"You guessed it."

"Listen to this. One of the PNAC's main members--Paul Wolfowitz--created the Office of Special Plans. He continues to make plans and strategies for the war in Iraq. He's submitted dozens of proposals to the OSP. And this is the same guy who's now running the World Bank."

"It's scary to think that the person controlling the world's money is also planning war."

"Hollywood could not script a better movie with a better bad-guy. Just listen to his name, Wolf – Foe – Witz. It just sounds evil."

Daniel almost cracked a smile at the line, but his straight-laced personality refrained from showing too much emotion.

"I had a question about PNAC," said Nathan. "How is President Bush involved with it?"

"George W.," said Daniel trying to mimic the president's Texas accent. "He's not officially a member of PNAC, but he's close with the organization. If all the PNAC members were brothers and sisters, President Bush would be a cousin."

"So he'll listen to them. Like he listened to them when they proposed a New Pearl Harbor, aka 9/11."

"Somewhat, but 9/11 is not quite that simple. Remember there are several reasons why 9/11 happened. PNAC breathing down Bush's neck about going to war in the Middle East was just one of the issues. The masterminds in PNAC were able to plan the "New Pearl Harbor," but it was Bush and his administration who used this event to kill several birds with one stone. Bush is actually a lot smarter than most think."

Nathan recalled the four major reasons that Daniel had talked about the night before. "Going back to the four reasons behind 9/11, you said you were going to tell me more about the second reason--oil and energy. Is it the fact that 9/11 gave Bush a chance to get a foothold in Middle Eastern oil?"

"Yes, but once again, it's not quite that simple. You've only scratched the surface. You'll need to do some more research to understand the complete picture regarding the oil and energy issues. I'll try to send you an email with some info about this tonight."

Nathan could not help from laughing. "More facts and figures?"

"What are you laughing at?"

"You--you've been talking nonstop about 9/11 info since I met you. You're like a walking encyclopedia."

"Sorry, I haven't spoken that much in the last five years. I guess I'm just excited that I have someone to talk to. From now on, I'll try not to bore you by trying to explain every detail from five year's worth of research."

"No, please do. I want to know everything you know. I'll try to wrap my head around all the facts and figures as best as I can."

"Maybe it'd help if I threw in a joke every once in a while," said Daniel in his American accent that had hints of Israeli dialect. "How about this one--What is PNAC's favorite NFL football team?"

"What?"

"The New York Jets." For the first time, Daniel showed his teeth in a smile. "Get it--Twin Towers in New York, two jets on 9/11."

Nathan could only smile at the corny joke. "I take that back--you can stick to being a human encyclopedia quoting lists of facts and figures. Let's just try to take it one step at a time. I may've graduated from Yale, but I don't have an IQ that's off the charts like you." Nathan paused and looked at the large stacks of files that contained Daniel's research. "Just tell me if I get on your nerves. As a journalist, I'm used to asking a lot of questions."

"You won't be bothering me as long as you trust what I'm saying. I know I'm throwing a lot of heavy information at you really fast, so please slow me down and ask questions if you're unsure about anything."

Speaking of questioning," said Nathan. "Earlier today, I was asking a friend who writes for *Time* magazine about the current state of corporate media. He said that every major media outlet is owned by one of five major conglomerates."

"That's the state of freedom of the press in this country. Ninety percent of mainstream media is under the control of five corporations--five corporations that only care about making money."

"My friend said it was difficult writing for a bureaucratic corporation. As journalists, we were taught in college to report the news just as it happens. Now, he's had to learn to write stories based on what the executives dictate."

"And these 'stories' are what the American people believes."

"It makes you wonder who you can trust." Nathan paused for a second to look Daniel in the eye. "Just out of curiosity--why do you trust me?"

"I saw you were investing a lot of time viewing 9/11 sites from your office. I knew you were either sparking an interest for the truth or trying to suppress it."

"What do you mean you saw what websites I was viewing?"

"You forget I have access to Akamai's servers. I navigated around the cache servers to see where you've been on the Internet."

"You're telling me that you monitor all the Internet activity at the Pentagon?"

"No, I couldn't do that even if I had a team of 1,000 helping me. I found you by setting up a filter that catches anyone from the Pentagon who visits certain 9/11 sites."

"Why would you set something like that up?"

"There are several Pentagon employees who've been hired to create their own 9/11 conspiracy theories. They post comments and create websites that feature conspiracies which can be easily disproved. They also create stories that are so absurd that it brings a bad name to 9/11 conspiracies."

"I know what you're talking about. We have some people in the OSP who have been assigned the same task with anti-war sites. I think it's called 'poisoning-the-well.' You basically agree with the group or idea, but you take it to the extreme so that you are actually adding 'poison' to a good source of information. Some OSP personnel spend the entire day on Internet discussion boards and chat rooms using this poisoning-the-well strategy to suppress anti-war sentiment. And this is only one of their techniques; they use dozens of different mindgames to control the anti-war movement."

"Disinformation agents use the same strategies with 9/11 conspiracies," said Daniel. "Some of the stories they've posted are just ridiculous. They've claimed that Jews were responsible for the 9/11 attacks. They've said that energy beams from satellites were used to weaken the Twin Towers' structure. Some websites have gone so far as to state that planes were taken over by electromagnetic waves from UFO spaceships."

"Thus making the general public associate conspiracy theories with people who have mental problems," added Nathan.

"Exactly. Anyway, when I saw you were not poisoning-the-well or playing any other mindgames in the Information War, I checked out your background and discovered you have a spotless record. You're known as a man of integrity, and your superiors think highly of you. I then stumbled across your wife's suspicion prior to 9/11. You seemed to be like the perfect person who would want to help me."

"You picked the right man. I'll do whatever it takes to expose who murdered Cindy." He paused. "And the other thousands of people who have died because of these corrupt, power hungry maniacs who want to control the world." He met Daniel's eyes. "They've got to be stopped."

"This can be done. All we have to do is expose the truth to the world."

Chapter 16

3211 Fourth Street NE
September 16, 2006
6:00 a.m.

Nathan set his coffee mug next to the keyboard. Even on a Saturday morning, there was no sleeping in for him.

He opened the latest email Daniel had sent him.

Subject: #2 Oil/Energy
From: DL@boc.ix
To: T.Ruth@boc.ix
Date: 9/16/06

T.Ruth,

Here are some facts and figures about oil and energy you need to know before going any further.

• The U.S. consumes over 20 million barrels of oil every day. Of that 20 million, 15 million comes from foreign providers. PNAC knew that it would be impossible to achieve "global dominance" if the U.S. was dependent on other nations for energy. In fact, the same PNAC report written in 2000 that called for a "New Pearl Harbor" also recommended gaining control of Middle Eastern oil fields.

• *Iraq has the second largest oil reserves in the world. At the time, Afghanistan was planning to build a key oil pipeline. Having ties to this pipeline would be a strategic way to have a hand in the world's oil distribution.*

• *President Bush is close friends with Saudi Arabian oil men. If fact, the Saudis were one of the main contributors to Bush's presidential campaign. Saudi businessmen have donated approximately $1.5 billion to the Bush family and their businesses over the last 25 years.*

• *President Bush's best friends in America (from his home state of Texas) are involved in oil (as you recall, Bush himself used to have a career in the oil industry). Along with their riches, Texas oil men have a lot of power. They use their power to influence every sphere of American life.*

It seems there's a conference held near my hotel tonight, and all the rooms are booked. I don't want to put you at risk, but spending a night at your place would take care of where I'm going to sleep tonight. Plus, it will give me a chance to further explain the oil/energy issue with you. I'll be at the usual spot this afternoon.

Sincerely,
D L

That afternoon, Nathan traveled to the warehouse to meet Daniel. He tried opening the door, but it was locked. He knocked.

Seconds later the door squeaked open. A rat took the opportunity to squeeze through the opening, passing between Nathan's feet. Nathan jumped, his voice reacting to the surprise, "Whoa!"

"Shhh. Not so loud," Daniel whispered from the doorway. "There are people around here during the daytime."

Nathan lowered his voice as he entered the warehouse. "Sorry, rats are my greatest fear." Nathan surveyed the dusty warehouse. Even during the daytime, it remained fairly dark. "You want to go to my place?"

"Is it safe?"

"Yes, it's out in the suburbs. No one will come by except my teenage daughter."

Daniel put on a Boston Red Sox hat and a pair of sunglasses. He tossed a large backpack over his shoulder. "Okay, let's go."

Before exiting the building, Daniel cracked the warehouse door and peeked outside. After he studied the surroundings, the two walked to the corner. Again at the corner, Daniel checked both ways. "Where did ya park?"

"In a public parking garage on the opposite side of the hotel." Nathan nodded to his right. "It's another block away."

"The garage will have video surveillance. Why don't you go get the car and pick me up here on the corner?"

"Sure, I'll be right back." Nathan was starting to have concerns about bringing Daniel back to his house. Though he trusted Daniel, he was not sure if he was ready to take on the responsibility of spreading the truth about 9/11 to the world.

Nathan pulled his Crown Victoria up to the curve. Daniel wasted no time in getting in.

"Are you always this paranoid?"

"Nathan, think about it--basically I'm an Israeli spy who's supposed to be dead. I'm using my software company to illegally hack into government information so I can gain incriminating evidence about a group who will do anything to gain more power. I don't want to be paranoid, but I also do not want to endanger either of our lives."

"I see your point." Nathan looked into his rearview mirror as he changed lanes.

Daniel saw the movement and asked, "Do you know how to identify government cars? Obviously you know to look for white and black Crown Vics like this one, but you should also look out for black Chevrolet SUVs."

"Yeah, I know."

Daniel strapped on his seatbelt. "So, what did you think of that information I sent you in this last email?"

"I knew about the American dependence on oil, but I had no idea Bush was so close with Saudi Arabian millionaires."

"With Bush in office, the Saudi aristocrats have as much influence over American democracy as American citizens."

"Let me guess--they also fueled 9/11. No pun intended."

"Somewhat. Their influence in the White House was one of the main reasons 9/11 was carried out."

Nathan gave Daniel a puzzled look.

"Let me explain. You've probably had a lot of questions on why the U.S. planned an attack on the Pentagon. The collapse of the Twin Towers was enough to give PNAC the 'New Pearl Harbor' that they needed, right?"

"I've been questioning that a lot in the past two days. Why did the Pentagon have to be attacked as well?"

"That's a good question--one that many from the Truth Movement haven't asked." Daniel paused to clear his throat. "Basically, the Bush administration wanted to destroy evidence housed at the Pentagon. Not only evidence, but the people who knew about this evidence as well."

Nathan stared at the road in front of him, his mind racing with memories. "Before work that day, Cindy said she had to be at a mandatory meeting with other members of the Department of Intelligence."

"More than likely, bombs were placed in that exact room."

"Bombs?"

"The 757--or should I say missile--was just a smokescreen. Bombs were placed inside the Pentagon to get rid of the information the government needed to hide. The bombs destroyed the evidence, and the missile destroyed the evidence of detonative devices being used."

Nathan pounded his fist into the steering wheel, accidentally hitting his horn. "Why didn't I see this before? As I was evacuating the building, my friend Robert said he smelled Cordite--the principle explosive used in many bombs. I asked him if he was sure, and he said that there was no doubt--that he'd always remember that smell from his service in the Gulf War. For a minute, I thought we were being bombed, but later, when I heard it was an airplane, I didn't think about it again."

Daniel nodded. "It's amazing how the media makes us blind."

"And the bombs--I felt them go off just before the missile hit. I was on the floor for about a second, then I heard the whistling noise that caused the second explosion."

"The first explosion was undoubtedly the bombs going off."

"And you think the bombs were set off to kill all those who may have accidentally come across PNAC's plan."

"Not only those who found out about it--but also those who helped PNAC carry out the attacks. To create this "New Pearl Harbor," several agencies would've had to been in on this. I'm guessing that PNAC created a special committee--9/11 consultants, if you will--to make sure there'd be no hindrances in carrying out their plan."

Their conversation had lasted long enough to bring the pair to Nathan's home. Daniel glanced out the window as he finished speaking, his eyes instinctively searching the area around Nathan's house.

Nathan took no notice of Daniel's suspicion. "Do you think Cindy was on this committee of 9/11 consultants?"

"Not really. From her last email, we know she knew something, but it didn't sound like she was involved in any of the planning--the email sounded like she just had suspicion from something she had come across." Daniel watched the garage door slowly rise. "I'm assuming that if anyone from the Pentagon would've stumbled across PNAC's plot, it would've been someone from the Department of Intelligence like your wife."

"Trust me, no one was more meticulous than Cindy. If something wasn't right--she would've been the one to spot it." Nathan put the car in park, but made no movement to get out. "What do you think she spotted--what information could she have come across?"

"I don't know." Daniel looked toward the door of the house. "I was hoping she may've left something here at the house--a computer disk, a note, or some sort evidence."

Chapter 17

3211 Fourth Street NE
September 16, 2006
12:30 p.m.

Nathan and Daniel searched boxes in the attic where Nathan had saved all of Cindy's old things. They hoped to come across some kind of clue behind she may've left behind.

"So you believe all those not in PNAC who had prior knowledge about 9/11 were somehow killed on 9/11?" asked Nathan, as he searched through a box that contained many photographs.

"Yes. The top perpetrators knew that they had to get rid of any whistleblowers who could later expose the truth. So they plotted to kill anyone who could trace 9/11 back to the government--including me who was supposed die on 9/11 with Cindy and the rest."

Nathan stopped digging through the box and raised his eyebrow.

Daniel picked up on his unasked question. "They knew I had access to Akamai's servers and could get into Pentagon files. The night before 9/11, I got a call from a prospective client who requested that I take the first flight out of Boston to LA. To this day, I've never found out who made that call."

"But someone else knew enough to warn you not to take that flight."

"Yes. Thankfully, I got the call from someone in airport security, warning me to get off the plane immediately. At the time, I had no clue what was going on. But I'm glad I took heed to the warning. I just regret that I was unable to tell the other passengers that something suspicious was going on." Daniel paused to look at some of the things in the drawer. "I wasn't the only one who had access to the Pentagon's computer infrastructure on that flight."

"How do you know this? Did you know any of the others on the flight?"

"One--Jeff Mladenik. He was president of an IT firm called E-Logic. E-Logic partnered with Akamai to install software and Intranet networks on Pentagon computers. And there were several others I didn't know who were on that plane because they once had access to Pentagon computers. Christopher Zarba worked for Concord Communications. Concord is a highly-respected IT firm that frequently does work at the Pentagon. Edmund Glazer, the CFO of MRV Communications, was also murdered for what he had access to. His company provides integrated solutions and fiber optic networks to the Pentagon."

"They put all of you on the same plane?"

"I'm just getting started," replied Daniel in a firm tone. "Dozens of other individuals on that flight probably knew something suspicious was going on at the Pentagon. Multiple upper level members from Raytheon, the company that manufactures the Global Hawk aerial vehicles, were on the flight. Several Pentagon employees were scattered across the four hijacked flights. Some of their jobs at the Pentagon were so classified that I've been unable to find their official title--I just know they were analysts for top secret affairs. And then there was John O'Neil."

Nathan's head turned upon hearing the name he recognized. "The FBI agent, right? The one who was an al-Qaeda expert."

"If anyone knew al-Qaeda's involvement in 9/11--it would've been him. But because he knew too much, he was fired from the FBI. He was ordered to start a new job with WTC security on the day before 9/11. Conveniently, he died in the South Tower during the attacks."

"I guess it was a genius plan--PNAC killed everyone who knew the truth about the attacks. Now the only ones left who know what really happened are the PNAC members and top government officials who would only be incriminating themselves if they tried to come out with the truth."

"I believe there's someone from the government who's trying to get the truth out. He's leaving breadcrumbs for people like me who are seeking for the answers. It's been like trying to put together a jigsaw puzzle, but I'm just about finished. All that's left are those two or three pieces in the center."

For the next three hours, Nathan and Daniel searched through computer disks, post cards, and anything that Cindy could have left behind as evidence. Their search provided no luck. However, during this time, Daniel was able to explain how PNAC was able to carry out the attacks, despite the fact that all the members of "9/11 consulting committee" were killed that day.**

The two eventually took a break to grab a bite to eat. Nathan cooked a pot of soup while Daniel continued to roll out facts and figures from his research.

"Tell me more about how oil and energy was involved," Nathan said, stirring the pot of soup on the stove.

"Nathan, do you remember what I was telling you earlier about Bush's rich friends in Saudi Arabia and Texas?"

"That they're in the oil business?"

"Exactly. 'Black Gold' has made them very rich and very powerful. In many ways, they're more powerful than the president. As long as they work together to control the world's energy supply, these billionaires will have more power and money than you could imagine--enough power and money to get whatever they want."

"So you're saying the oil executives collaborate with each other to influence politics?"

"Yes. The American and Saudi Arabian oil oligopoly work together. I call them the 'oil mob.' They're 100 times more powerful than Al Capone's boys. Do you know why Bush won the state of Florida in the 2000 election?"

Nathan stared, obviously waiting.

"Let's just say his friends in Texas had something to do with it."

"Without the help of this 'oil mafia,' Bush wouldn't have become president?"

Daniel nodded in agreement. "They wanted Bush in the White House--they're good friends with him and his father. Besides, do you think the oil mob would've let the global-warming, anti-oil-consuming Al Gore become president?"

Nathan smiled. "I see your point." He stopped to reflect for a second. "I understand what you're saying about the 'oil mob' having so much power--but how are they involved in 9/11?"

"The oil mafia wasn't involved in planning or carrying out the attacks. They just influenced them. They used their power to get a president--Bush--in the White House who they could manipulate. In return, Bush used 9/11 to accommodate the oil mafia's agenda. I could talk for hours on how 9/11 has helped the oil businessmen--Dick Cheney and Halliburton, the value of the dollar, increased profits for every major oil corporation, Peak oil..."

"And don't forget the reason why we're fighting a war in the Middle East--to gain control of Iraqi oil."

"Precisely. Oil is the blood of this nation. America could not live without it. By gaining those oil sources in Iraq, America will no longer be as dependent on other countries for energy. PNAC wanted this oil, but they knew the American public would not go to war to get it."

"But after the 'false flag terrorist attack' and the patriotism created by 9/11, every American wanted to go to war."

"In theory, Bush made everyone happy by letting 9/11 happen. PNAC got their war in the Middle East. His power-hungry friends in the oil business got even richer and more powerful by rising oil prices and gaining Iraqi oil. And America gained enough oil reserves to ensure we'll have enough fuel to fill up our 6 miles-per-gallon SUVs."

Note: For an alternate version of this chapter (the original version was too "edgy" to publish), please visit the book's website at: www.AmTruth.com

** Also on the www.AmTruth.com website is Nathan and Daniel's conversation regarding how the 9/11 attacks were executed.

Chapter 18

3211 Fourth Street NE
September 16, 2006
3:15 p.m.

Over the course of lunch, Daniel explained motive Number
3 of 9/11--the influence on the American and global economies.
Many American corporations were able to profit greatly. Most
of these businesses had close ties with the oil industry, the
financial markets, and/or the government.

Their conversation eventually turned into a discussion of
how controlled explosives took down the Twin Towers and
World Trade Center 7.

"I've come across a lot of websites that suggest the Twin
Towers collapsed as a result of a controlled demolition," said
Nathan. "Is this theory true?"

"I'm not a structural engineer, but I believe the scientists and
physicists who have hypothesized the 'controlled demolition
theory' are correct."

"You don't think the plane collisions were not enough to
take down the Towers?"

"Not at all. The architects of the buildings have said that
they built the Towers to withstand the force of a commercial
jetliner crashing into them. And you can tell by the way they
came down that it was not from structural damage. I'm sure
you've seen the footage dozens of times."

Nathan nodded, remembering the video clips that inundated
the 9/11 truth websites.

"In the footage, you'll see that the towers fall straight down," said Daniel using his hand as a demonstration. "They did not lean--or fall in the direction in which the plane flew in. They fall straight down into their own footprint--just as it's done in a controlled demolition."

"I'm assuming controlled demolition crews make the buildings fall straight down to prevent damaging anything in the vicinity."

Daniel nodded. "Several controlled demolition experts have said that the collapse of 9/11 was a work of art from a demolition perspective."

Nathan's face tightened.

"I know, it sounds atrocious to think of it in such a way. But it's the truth--many demolition crews admit that they couldn't take down the buildings in the same manner as it happened on 9/11." Daniel took a bite of his soup. "You also have to look at how fast the Towers came down."

"The clips on the Internet show the Towers collapsing in 10 seconds."

"10 seconds--that's nearly freefall speed," exclaimed Daniel. "Meaning if I dropped a ball from the top, it'd take 10 seconds for it to reach the ground traveling at the speed of gravity. This fact discredits the government's latest theory on the collapse."

"The pancake theory?"

"You're familiar with it?"

Nathan nodded. He had just covered the theory in his latest report to the media. It was the idea that the areas impacted by the planes collapsed first, then the weight of these floors caused the floor beneath them to collapse, which started a chain reaction all the way down.

"The only problem with the Pancake Theory," said Daniel, "is that it would've taken much longer than 10 seconds for the entire building to collapse. Taking friction and inertia into consideration, scientists have stated it'd take at least half of a second for each floor to collapse. If the building started collapsing on the 90th floor, it would've taken the Towers a minimum of 45 seconds to collapse."

"There's another government theory I wrote about--that fires from the jet fuel took down the Towers."

"Yes, but this is ridiculous. Fire cannot take down a steel framed building. No other steel frame building has collapsed from fire--in all of architectural history! Last year, a fire in the Windsor Tower in Madrid, Spain raged for over fourteen hours, but still the building didn't collapse. There's no way a fire on the 80th floor that only burned for an hour could have taken down a 110-story steel framed skyscraper."

"I was reading an article that said the fires were not even hot enough to do much damage," stated Nathan.

"By looking at the fire's color, firefighters could tell that it was oxygen deprived. They speculate the fires only reached 1200°F. However, we can see molten metal running down the exterior of the Towers just before their collapse. A minimum of 2700°F is needed to melt structural steel. Obviously, there was something else producing this molten metal."

"Possibly thermite?" asked Nathan, finishing his bowl of soup.

"Yes, thermite as an incendiary agent can reach temperatures up to 6500°F. If explosive material containing thermite was strategically placed in key areas throughout the Towers, it could've easily brought down the Towers."

Nathan tried wrapping his head around the details. "6500°F, inertia, molten steel--you're starting to sound like a walking encyclopedia again."

Daniel smiled. "I'm just getting started. I've basically memorized the hundreds pages of research I've done on the Towers."

"Well, tell me this..." said Nathan, thinking he'd come upon a flaw in Daniel's theory. "How were these thermite bombs placed throughout the Towers? Wouldn't someone be suspicious of crews hauling large explosive devices through their offices?"

"You've got a good point. Normally, you couldn't sneak huge explosives into the building without someone taking notice. However, on the weeks preceding 9/11, the Twin Towers were running evacuation drills. Entire floors had to vacate the building. Not only were they evacuated, but certain floors had their power cut off for extended times."

"They prevented entire offices from working?"

"Yes, and do you know who ran the security firm that called for these evacuations?"

"Who?"

"Securacom. A company headed by Marvin Bush and Wirt Walker--President Bush's brother and cousin.

"Another too-random coincidence." Nathan took his bowl to the dishwasher. "One website I visited showed proof of explosives being set off just before the collapse."

"Yes--the squibs. Just before the Towers collapsed, plumes of smoke erupted from lower floors. The squibs came out in succession--as if it was a time-delay sequence." Daniel handed Nathan his bowl to put in the dishwasher. "Not only is there video footage that shows these squibs, but firefighters and eyewitnesses also admit hearing a sequence of explosions. They admit hearing 'pops' and 'booms' and seeing bright flashes--all of which are indicative of thermite explosive devices."

"And the same thing happened for WTC 7, right?"

"WTC 7 is probably the strongest evidence of a controlled demolition. Many people forget that this 47-story building across the street also collapsed. It was never hit by any plane, but it still collapsed."

"The reports I wrote for the Pentagon said that fires from the Twin Towers took it down."

"And we've already discussed how fires alone could not take down a steel frame building. Plus, you have to take into consideration that WTC 7 wasn't even the closest building to the Twin Towers. Several other buildings were just as close, and they didn't collapse."

"It makes you wonder why WTC 7 collapsed."

"There's no question why it collapsed. WTC 7 held offices for the CIA, FBI, SEC, the secret service, and the Pentagon. There was something in these offices that the government wanted to hide."

"Any idea of what it could be?"

Daniel shook his head. "No clue. I've searched and searched but can't find any of the WTC 7 archives. I'm pretty sure that the SEC computers would've shown evidence of the insider trading on Wall Street occurring before 9/11. But I also think there was something else--something that was worth 3,000 lives."

"What about the Twin Towers--do you think they also held top secret information?"

"No, they were just the 'New Pearl Harbor.' They were the perfect candidate. They were two landmarks located in one of the most popular places in the world. Besides, the owner of the Towers--Larry Silverstein--wanted to take them down."

"If they were popular landmarks, why would Silverstein want to take them down?"

"They cost more money than they were worth. The gigantic Towers were getting old, and they were requiring a lot of maintenance. Silverstein had just completed millions in renovations, and he needed to spend millions more in removing asbestos. He even hired a firm to give him a quote for how much it'd cost to take them down."

"How much would it cost?"

"Nearly $15 billion. That's based on taking the building down floor-by-floor. Since it was in a highly-populated area, controlled demolition was not an option."

"So Silverstein was in on 9/11?"

"Silverstein has plenty of friends in Washington. I'm sure one of the PNAC guys knew his situation, and they made him an offer he could not refuse. Silverstein is a businessman— it'd be foolish of him to spend $15 billion to take down the Towers when he could earn $5 billion in insurance claims from 'terrorist attacks.'"

"Sounds like a smart move on Silverstein's part."

"Silverstein might have business smarts, but he doesn't have common sense. In an interview after 9/11, he admitted that he ordered to take down WTC 7. His exact words were 'to pull it,' which is demolition lingo for a controlled demolition. He later stated that he did not mean 'pull it' in a demolition manner. Then what manner did he mean 'pull it'?" Daniel added, sarcastically. "To use pickup trucks to 'pull it' out of the way?"

For the rest of the afternoon, the two discussed more about the collapse of the Twin Towers. At first, it was a little complex for Nathan to understand, but as Daniel explained the logistics, everything fit together like pieces of a puzzle.

Eventually Nathan's daughter Claire came in, interrupting their conversation.

"Claire, where have you been?" asked her father.

"I went to the mall with Christen and Mary to look for some new jeans. We're going to a movie tonight. Is that okay?"

"Sure, just make sure to be back before midnight."

Claire's eyes turned to the slim man sitting in their kitchen.

"Claire, this is Daniel," Daniel gave Nathan a stern look when he used his real name. "Daniel…Smith, he's a buddy of mine from the Navy."

Claire extended her hand. "Nice to meet you."

"He's in town for a business conference. I told him he could stay with us while he's here." Nathan walked over to the pot of soup of the stove. "I have some soup left over, did you want a bowl?"

"No thanks, we ate at the mall," she said as she made her way to her room.

"You two seem fairly close," commented Daniel.

"We are. We've grown even closer this last year since my oldest moved to college. You have any kids?"

"Two sons." Daniel looked down, thinking of past memories. "Not seeing them has been the hardest part of the last five years.

I've wanted so desperately just to talk to them, but it'd be too risky to make contact. I hack into my wife's computer and check her email account every night to see if she has uploaded any recent pictures."

Nathan looked into Daniel's downcast eyes. "Daniel, this may seem odd to ask you this, but you don't seem... Jewish."

Daniel smiled. "What did you expect? That I'd be wearing the Star of David on my sleeve?"

"No," replied Nathan, laughing slightly. "But your accent, for example."

"I was born here in America. I grew up in Denver before my parents decided to move back to Israel. I moved to Boston in '96 to get my PhD from MIT. I've been here since."

"So, you're an American citizen?"

"Yes. And even though I was heavily involved with the Israeli military, I'm still proud to consider myself an American."

"The Isreali government let an American citizen join their secret Special Forces unit?"

"I have a dual-citizenship. And I was recruited to be in Sayeret Markal because of my computer skills--not to be a spy. Besides, do you know how many dual-citizens are in the U.S. government and military?"

"Come to think of it, I do remember several in the navy who were dual-citizens."

"Speaking of being in the military," said Daniel. "Why did you enlist in the Navy? No offense, but you've never struck me as the military type."

"I'm not. That's why I've being doing paperwork and media relations at the Pentagon for the last 20 years. I enlisted in the Navy because it was important to my father that I follow family tradition, but I only stayed in active service for a couple years." Nathan pinched the small portion of fat around his midsection. "Sitting behind a desk on a daily basis has added 15 pounds worth of baggage that I didn't have back then. I've tried to keep in shape, though. I run or lift weights nearly every day, but I can no longer run marathons like I used to."

The rest of that weekend the two plotted how they were going to tell the world the truth. Nathan would use his contacts with the media, and Daniel would explain his documented research. Nathan even gave Daniel a lesson on how to conduct a press conference where he wouldn't sound like a human encyclopedia.

"We're going do this, Nathan. If you can help me get some more inside information from the Pentagon, everything will be complete."

"I'll do whatever it takes to tell the world the truth."

Daniel's eyes gave Nathan one-hundred percent of their attention. "Do you mean that? What if you're caught--would you tell them about me or my research?"

"No. I promise I'll never rat you out."

Daniel stood from his seat and used his hands to project his emotion. "I need more than a promise to never 'rat me out.' I need you committed to this, even if you're life is on the line."

Nathan stood eye-to-eye to meet Daniel. "My wife was murdered because she knew something about a government conspiracy. Nearly 3,000 individuals were murdered so PNAC could push their agenda. Hundreds of thousands of Iraqis have been killed in war, even though no weapons of mass destruction have been found. I'm going to make sure that it stops here."

Daniel patted him on his shoulder, "That's all I needed to hear."

Chapter 19

The Pentagon - OSP
September 18, 2006
10:22 a.m.

Nathan took a break from work to pull up his boc.ix account. He felt a little insecure about checking his emails from his office, despite the fact Daniel assured him that it could not be traced. He glanced out his office, making sure no one was coming his way.

In his mailbox, he saw a new email from Daniel.

Subject: Key Contact
From: DL@boc.ix
To: T.Ruth@boc.ix
Date: 9/18/06

T.Ruth,

There's a figure at the Pentagon you should meet. His name is Shawn K. Coleman. He worked in the White House during 9/11, but has been recently moved to the Office of Management & Budget in the Pentagon (stationed at 2B155).Normally, I wouldn't recommend you talking to any other government employee about 9/11, but my sources tell me Coleman is very upset with the Bush Administration.

Also, I just wanted to let you know that I'll be back in my usual position. I think it's best if we keep separate.

Sincerely,
D L

Nathan hit *reply*.

Yes. It's probably a good idea that we're not together. I'd like to spend the next day or two studying more about what we've covered so far. We're on the verge of bringing to light the biggest conspiracy in American history – I want to make sure I know my stuff for when I'm in front of the press.

I also had a question for you that we have not covered yet:
How is Osama bin Laden involved with 9/11?

Keep me posted,
T.Ruth

Nathan called Shawn Coleman's secretary and scheduled to meet him over lunch. Nathan used the excuse that his boss had ordered him to talk with him about a budget increase for the OSP.

The two met for lunch in the center of the Pentagon in an open courtyard. Green grass, late-blooming flowers, and comfortable benches filled this oasis from the office. Even after 20 years at the Pentagon, it was hard for Nathan to believe this tranquil plaza was surrounded by the thousands of tons of infrastructure that housed the center of war.

After grabbing a hot dog at The Ground Zero Café, the two talked about business and budget estimates. Nathan eventually changed subjects. "What do you think of the 9/11 Conspiracy Theories that saturate the Internet?"

"I don't know. I've just tried to ignore them. President Bush told us to brush aside anything that could shift the blame in bringing justice to those who deserve it."

"You're not worried that there may be some truth in them?"

"I'm more worried about the Patriot Act," said Shawn.

"What about it?"

"It basically gives the government dictatorship power by taking away our Constitutional rights," said Shawn with an increased emotion in his voice. "But what really bothers me is that it was written before 9/11."

"Before 9/11?"

"Think about it--there's no way they could've put the Patriot Act together in 45 days."

Nathan thought about the amount of work it'd take to put together a piece of legislation over 300 pages. His experience in writing government documents had taught him how much time and attention went into something of this nature. He knew it should've taken months to complete.

"It was not only written in 45 days," continued Coleman. "But it was passed through both houses of Congress as well. Many congressmen admit that they didn't even get a chance to read it."

Nathan's tempered flared when he realized what this meant. *Congress did not even know they were giving away every American's rights.*

When Nathan got home from work, he opened his email to give Daniel a summary of his conversation with Shawn. In his mailbox, he saw he had two emails--one from an address he did not know. *Certainly a secure email address will not receive spam.* He opened Daniel's email first to see if it explained why he got an email from another source.

Subject: Re:Re: Key Contact
From: DL@boc.ix
To: T.Ruth@boc.ix
Date: 9/13/06

T.Ruth,

Osama bin Laden? Good question.
He was not at all behind 9/11. Contrary to what is reported
in the media, the U.S. actually has a good relationship with
al-Qaeda. The U.S. has been secretly funding al-Qaeda
operations for decades.

It is true that al-Qaeda is behind many of the
world's major terrorist attacks. The U.S. does not
support these terrorist attacks, but by giving al-
Qaeda money, al-Qaeda does not to attack the U.S.
("Don't bite the hand that feeds you" philosophy).

Bin Laden and al-Qaeda were actually the perfect
group to blame for 9/11. They were in the Middle
East (makes PNAC happy by going to war there),
plus they were Muslims who were already guilty of
heinous crimes. Since the vast majority of Americans
are Christians, having radical Muslims kill our
innocent citizens was the ultimate act of hatred.

From movies and television, Americans have
learned that there is always a "bad guy." The U.S.
government knows this psychological fact, and they
made sure that the "bad guy" from 9/11 was the
most heinous evil-villain that they could find. Osama
bin Laden was the perfect character for the part.

I first started looking into al-Qaeda when a media
report said they planned their terrorists' attacks
over the Internet. Like most mainstream media
reports, this was bullshit. There's nothing on the
Internet that the U.S. cannot track. If you thought I
can pull off amazing stuff on the Net, this is nothing
compared to what the MIT grads now at the Pentagon
can do. The U.S. government (not Al Gore) invented

the Internet. Since it's beginning, they've used it to gather the information they want. They not only know where Osama bin Laden is sending his Internet communications from, but they know when he lifts his fingers off the keyboard to pick his nose.

Sincerely,
D L

P.S. Check the FBI's most wanted list. Osama bin Laden is on there, but the 9/11 attacks are not mentioned in the crimes he is charged with. Even the FBI does not have enough evidence to say bin Laden is to blame for 9/11.

Nathan glanced at the other email. He saw it was from government address. He reluctantly opened it.

Subject: URGENT: From the Office of U.S. Intelligence
From: Adam.Eveland@state.gov
To: T.Ruth@boc.ix
Date: 9/13/06

YOUR LIFE IS IN JEOPARDY!!! The gentlemen who you have been meeting is not who he says he is.

I will wait until I can talk to you in person until I go into specifics.

I purpose to meet at the Lincoln Memorial tonight at 9:00 p.m. It's a public place that will be secure. I will be wearing dark clothing.

Regards,
Adam Eveland

An unsettling feeling started in his stomach, then ran throughout his body. His suspicion he first felt about this hooded figure may have been correct. *Who is this Daniel? A government official who's making sure I don't know too much? Or a criminal who's been misleading me from the start?*

Nathan looked at the email address--one given only to federal employees. Nathan had many friends at the Pentagon, maybe one of them was looking out for him.

Chapter 20

Lincoln Memorial
September 18, 2006
9:00 p.m.

Nathan examined the back of a five-dollar bill in the dim light. Raising his eyes, he studied the real structure in front of him. He climbed the stairs to the massive Abraham Lincoln statute situated behind the white columns. Even though this popular tourist attraction was open to until midnight, only one young couple had come to view the statue on this chilly fall night.

Nervously, Nathan scanned the area. Chill bumps broke out on his skin, and they weren't from the cold night's air. He stepped into a well-lit portion of the marble building, hoping the brightness would calm his racing pulse.

He turned when he reached the light, again scanning the area Lincoln dominated. Slowly, a figure wearing dark clothing emerged from the edge of the statue, coming into view.

With his heart still beating rapidly, Nathan approached the small figure. "Adam?"

"Yes," answered a female voice.

Nathan was taken off guard. He squinted into the dim light and saw long hair under a knit cap. "Sorry. I didn't expect—"

"A woman? Does that make a difference?"

"No," said Nathan, his body still tense. "I just want to know what's going on."

Adam began pacing slowly; Nathan followed by her side. "You're being misled. The person you've been talking to is not who he says he is."

"Who is he?"

"A known terrorist."

Nathan shook his head in disbelief. He could not believe that he of all people had been misled by a total stranger. "It's just that he looks so much like the man he claims to be."

"And who is that?" asked Adam.

Nathan paused. He worried about telling her too much. Even if she was with the government, he did not want to incriminate himself for treachery. "He told me to call him DL. That he was an insider with information, and he'd like to keep it on the 'Down Low.'"

She nodded her head. "He's been known for using this alias."

"Why did you want to meet me here?"

"I knew your wife--I work in the Department of Intelligence. I greatly respected her, and she greatly respected you." Adam paused to look up at Lincoln. "We're one step away from busting this guy. When we do, we'll be forced to arrest you for being an accomplice. We could even find you guilty of treason."

"I've done nothing!" objected Nathan. "I've only met with this so-called terrorist."

"I know. It's obvious from your record that you're not a terrorist. That's why I wanted to meet with you privately. You can prove your innocence by turning in this DL." Adam handed Nathan a tiny dot that was the width of a pencil's eraser. "GPS tracking device. Take it to your friend, and all charges against you will be dropped."

Nathan studied the chip and contemplated taking it to the warehouse. Suddenly, he remembered his emotionally-charged speech from the night before in which he promised never to turn in Daniel. *For this last week, have I been the mere pawn of a terrorist? But Daniel can't be a terrorist--he's never hinted of harm--he just wants the truth. But then again, he keeps mentioning how he needs top secret info from the Pentagon.* Nathan took a moment to examine his setting--very easily accessible, an odd place to hold a private meeting. *If Adam works at the Pentagon, why did she want to meet here instead of my office?*

Nathan stepped in front of Adam to face her in the eyes. "You said you knew my wife--I've been having a lot of questions lately. Do you know what kind of meeting she was at during the attacks?"

Adam shook her head. "The only time I saw her that morning was in the break room getting a cup of coffee."

Coffee? At that moment, Nathan knew something was not right. He looked closer into her eyes. "You saw her in the break room. Do you remember if she was carrying around that ugly orange coffee mug I gave to her before we got married."

The woman's eyes shifted up and to the left. "She had it with her every morning."

Nathan's eye shifted down. "Yeah, I wish I could've found it in the rubble." Nathan lifted the GPS, bringing attention back to it. "I was planning to meet DL tomorrow evening at 9:00. You can make the bust then."

"We'll have a team prepared."

"Is there anything else I need to know?"

"That's all for now. Just remember to have that tracking device on you at all times."

Nathan turned to the stairs. When he felt that he was good distance away, he dropped the chip. However, Adam had a trained eye, and she was able to see the move even in the darkness.

"Wait. You..."

Nathan sprinted for the stairs.

"Stop right there!" Adam put her sleeve up to her mouth. "He dropped the chip. Peter, he's headed your way."

Nathan looked over his shoulder and saw Adam talking into a communication device. He ran as fast as he could, taking the stairs two steps at a time.

Nick Shelton

As soon as his feet hit the last step, he turned and ran toward the reflecting pool that extended in front of the Memorial. Suddenly, two gunshots broke the night's silence. The bullets whistled by him, crashing into the cement a few feet from his ankles. Instinctively, Nathan veered away from the gunfire. He headed for the trees that surrounded the Memorial.

As he sprinted through the trees' dark shadows, thoughts flew through Nathan's mind. *My car is too risky. Where can I go?* He decided to head north toward the highway.

"Freeze!" yelled a male voice in the distance as Nathan emerged from the trees' canopy.

Nathan again made a sharp change of direction. He had had no doubt this agent was the backup Adam had called for. Nathan feared the whole complex was surrounded by federal agents. This agent was only a hundred feet away and quickly approaching. He knew that there'd be no way to escape if there was any more of them.

Nathan's feet hardly touched the ground. The Memorial lawn was neatly manicured like a golf course's fairway, providing the perfect running surface. Never before had Nathan moved so fast; still, the federal agent was closing the gap. Nathan lost track of Adam, but she was back there somewhere.

Nathan stopped when he reached the four-lane road that circled the Memorial. Glancing back, the headlight of a car outlined the agent in pursuit. He was now less than 75 feet away. His gun pointed straight at Nathan.

Without hesitation, Nathan ran in front of the oncoming traffic, attempting to cross the busy street. Brakes screeched and horns blew, but Nathan miraculously got to the other side unscathed. Upon reaching the other side of the street, he quickly turned to see traffic impeding the male agent's pursuit. Nathan tore off, trying to distance himself from the agents behind him.

He ran through a park with several baseball and softball fields. He passed through unlit areas where he knew it'd be difficult to spot him. A sharp pain was developing in his side from a cramp; his lungs were burning from inhaling the cold air--but he wasn't about to slow down.

He raced to the intersection of 23rd street and Highway 50. There, he spotted a Chevrolet truck stopped behind the traffic light. He jumped into its truck bed.

"What in the hell are you doing?" the owner of the truck shouted through his open window.

"I...need'a...ride," said Nathan, breathing so hard that he could barely talk. He fumbled frantically through his wallet to get his Pentagon clearance to the OSP. "I work...for a government agency."

"Where do you need to go?" said the man who now felt like he was in a *James Bond* movie.

Nathan looked back and did not see Adam or the male agent. "Just keep driving."

Nathan slumped down into the truck bed.

As they approached another busy intersection, Nathan spotted a taxi sitting next to the curb. As the truck decelerated to a stop, Nathan jumped out and waved a sign of thanks to the driver.

He scrambled into the taxi's backseat. "I need to get to my hotel on the corner of Ridgeway and Columbus Circle. And I'm in a hurry."

Chapter 21

Hampton Inn
September 18, 2006
9:45 p.m.

Nathan glanced over his shoulder as he entered the hotel. No agents were in sight. He felt a moment of relief, feeling assured he'd lost them back at the highway.

He hurried to the lobby's desk.

"Welcome to the Hampton Inn. How may I help you?" asked the attractive desk clerk. The tone of her voice did not match her friendly greeting. Nathan assumed it must've been his appearance--he was drenched with sweat and had picked some filth from the truck bed.

"I need a room for the night."

The female attendant squinted at the computer screen in front of her. "Would you like a room with two twin beds or a queen?"

"Um--it depends. Where are these vacant rooms?"

"There are three vacant rooms with twin beds on the third floor, and one with a queen on the fourth."

"That's it?"

"Well, the entire second floor is vacant, but we won't start occupying those rooms until the others are filled."

"Let me make a quick call."

Nathan stepped back and pretended to make a call from his cell phone. When the desk clerk turned her attention away from him, Nathan hurried to the stairs.

He went to the second floor and started pounding on the doors. "Daniel! Daniel! Are you in there?" He continued down the row of doors, knocking on each one. "Daniel, this is urgent, if you're in there…"

A door partially opened behind him. "How many times have I told you not to use my real name?" Daniel tried to keep his voice to a whisper, but couldn't. "Hurry, come in!"

Nathan rushed in.

"What the hell are you doing here?" Daniel demanded. "And don't you understand what it means to keep a low profile."

"They're on to us!"

"Who?"

"I don't know. It was a woman using the alias Adam Eveland--very slender, athletic build. I'm assuming a federal agent, probably FBI or CIA. She fired shots when I tried to flee," Nathan grew out of breath just trying to explain it. "There was another agent. Several were surrounding the Lincoln Memorial."

"Hold on." Daniel gestured with his hands to settle Nathan down. "Start from the top. What were you doing there?"

Nathan took a deep breath before starting his confession. "I got an email from someone at the Pentagon. They told me that you weren't who you said you were--that you were a terrorist."

"Nathan, after what we've talked—" Daniel started.

"It's just that all of this has happened really fast. She convinced me that she was Intell, and that she had worked with Cindy. She told me that you were using me to get inside information. I was afraid I didn't know your true identity."

"Did you tell her anything about me?" Daniel asked, his eyes squinting in frustration.

"No," Nathan quickly replied. "I don't think she even knew your name. She told me they were going to make a bust within the next few days. But she acted like they didn't know your location. They needed me to turn you in. I knew something was not right when she handed me a GPS locator. When she mentioned something about Cindy's coffee mug--I realized she was lying from the start. Cindy didn't drink coffee--she didn't even touch anything with caffeine in it."

"You said they fired shots? Where at?"

"As soon as I exited the memorial--right in front of the stairs."

"No. What trajectory were the shots fired at? Where would the bullets have hit you if they were on target?"

"They missed low. The bullets would've hit my legs if she aimed more to the left."

"A low trajectory. They didn't want you dead. They need you to get to me." Daniel spoke quietly, pondering his comments.

"Do you think they know who you are?"

"No. I doubt they even know I'm alive." Daniel's thick eyebrows furrowed forward as he tried to think. "I don't know how they would've had knowledge of our connection. Unless... Nathan, did you check your emails from work?"

"A couple times."

"Is your office under video surveillance?"

"There's only a few parts of the Pentagon that aren't."

Daniel sighed with frustration. "They must've picked up on us through there. I'm sure they read your screen from the camera." Daniel hurried to his laptop on this desk to see what Intelligence may have gathered from their email communications.

"But I didn't think a surveillance camera could pick up the words off my screen. The ones at gas stations usually don't even show a clear picture of a robber's face."

A thought hit Daniel as Nathan explained his rational. *Security cameras.* "The hotel's security will have you on tape. We're not safe here." Daniel slammed shut his laptop and started placing his things in his backpack. "We've got to go."

"Where?"

"I got to get all my stuff from the warehouse. We'll have to decide from there."

Nathan could sense Daniel's irritation. "I'm sorry. I had no idea..."

"No, I should've planned for something like this." Daniel headed to the door. "But this could not have happened at a worse time."

Chapter 22

1227 Ridgeway Ave.
September 18, 2006
10:22 p.m.

Nathan helped Daniel gather his notebooks and files in the corner of the warehouse. "Any plans on where we go from here?"

"Not exactly sure, but you're going to have to go back to the Pentagon tomorrow."

Nathan stopped in his place. "After what happened tonight? Are you kidding?"

"Nathan, the only reason I brought you into this was to get your help recovering Pentagon files. We have to utilize your Pentagon access before it's too late."

"It's already too late. They already know what I know."

"You said you thought they were federal agents. If they were CIA from Langley, there's a chance that nobody at the Pentagon knows about this yet."

"I can't rely on that. I'd be insane to go in there tomorrow."

Daniel stopped gathering his research to give Nathan his attention. "Nathan, you have to realize there's only a select few in the government who know the truth about 9/11. There's even fewer who have been assigned to cover it up." Daniel paused. "Last night, you told me you'd be committed to this until the end. This is one of the risks we're going to have to take. If you don't take this risk tomorrow morning, we may never have the chance of getting into the Pentagon again."

Nathan took several seconds to think. "Alright, I'll do it. But I'll probably come out with handcuffs around my wrists. With the Patriot Act, they could even torture me if they wanted."

"Relax, we're going to be smart with this. Even if you do get caught, you'll have nothing to give up."

"What do you mean?"

"After tonight, we're going to split up. You won't know where I am or what I plan to do. If you're caught, you'll have no information to share. If they don't believe you, demand a lie detector test. Following so far?"

Nathan nodded his head.

"Good. Now let me explain what I need from the Pentagon. There's a set of files there that contains the archives from the WTC 7 computers. I can get to these files from Akamai's servers, but I cannot open them because they have a password encryption on them."

"And you want me to get the password?"

"No, you couldn't. Nobody can. It's a 50-character sequence that changes every hour. The passwords are created by performing a mathematical operation to a computer's 25-digit Network Access Code, or NAC. All computers within the first two rings of the Pentagon have the same NAC, allowing anyone with Level 5 clearance to open these classified files."

"So, you want me to open these files from one of these computers?"

"No, I just need the NAC. I can solve the algorithm that will translate the NAC into the correct password. I'll show you how to find a computer's NAC on my laptop before we split up--it's actually fairly easy."

"So all I need to do tomorrow is get this 25-digit NAC?"

Daniel hesitated. "There's one more thing, but I'll tell you about it later. First, we must establish how we're going to communicate now since our other method has been compromised." Daniel grabbed a large mobile phone from his backpack and tossed it to Nathan. "Take this."

"A Blackberry? I already have a cell phone."

"Is it on you?"

Nathan took out his mobile phone from his pocket. Daniel immediately snatched it and turned it off. "It has GPS tracking." Daniel threw the phone down and crushed it by stomping it. "We'll need to get out of here soon in case your friends from the Lincoln thought of tracking you by your phone."

Nathan studied the Blackberry as they head for the door. "Does this get the Internet?"

"Anywhere you get cell phone coverage. I think it will be our best option for communication. In fact, you could text message the 25-digit NAC to me through that. We'll also set up a simple Gmail account in case we need to send long messages."

"You don't think it's too risky to use a public email account?"

"No, we just can't write our real names or anything that relates to 9/11."

As they exited the hideout, Nathan thought about what all this meant to his future. "After I steal the NAC, will I have to go into hiding permanently?"

Daniel nodded. "I also suggest you go to the bank tomorrow before going into the Pentagon. You need to take out all the savings you have before they freeze your accounts."

Nathan showed an expression of distrust.

"I can see how you may be a little wary of doing this. I know you've had some doubts about who I am tonight. Don't worry; I'm not a terrorist, and I'm not a con artist interested in taking your money. I just know from experience that you'll need all the money you can get. Things get very expensive when no one can know your real identity."

"My whole savings? Most of it is for my kids' college savings."

"I don't want to sound cold-hearted, but you're going to need that money more than your children. Speaking of that-- I'm hoping your daughter has someone she can stay with until we release our research to the public."

Nathan nodded. "Her grandmother lives in town." Nathan grew full of worry when he thought of leaving his daughter. "I'll call both of them tonight and arrange for Claire to stay over there."

"Don't worry," said Daniel, looking into the concerned father's eyes. "Once you get me the two things from the Pentagon, it'll only take a week to get all of my research together to go public."

Nathan took a deep breath. "And this other thing you want…?"

"I'll wait to go into specifics. But it's a file with the codename, 'The Re Con.'"

Chapter 23

The Pentagon - OSP
September 19, 2006
8:30 a.m.

Nathan walked through the entrance of the Pentagon. He slid his security card through the processor. He let out a sign of relief when it allowed him enter with no difficulty. Once inside, he quickly made his way to his office. All the way there, he scanned his surroundings, making sure no one was taking special interest in him.

He reached his office without any problems. He logged onto his computer and entered the email address Daniel had given him. *T.Ruth.Moore@gmail.com:*

T.Ruth,

Here's what you need to know.

First, you need to find the NAC from a Level 5 security zone. Any computer within the first two rings of the Pentagon should have the information we need. Please send me a text message with the 25 digits if you're able to get it.

Next, you'll need to find the file code-named "The Re Con." It was actually a top-secret folder stored at the P-gon until 9/11 destroyed it. However, I found out that the P-gon backs up all files on microfiche tape in the document storage room in the basement. Inventory last taken for the area destroyed on 9/11 was on November 22, 1998. So your 2nd task is to look through the microfiche files and find this classified document.

Lastly, attached to this email is a computer programming script. From any computer in the P-gon, this script can access the P-gon's security admin controls. With one click of the mouse, this program will sound the emergency evacuation alarm for all sectors in the P-gon. I'll let you decide if and when this is necessary.

Sincerely,
DL

Attachment: P-gon_Master_Alarm.exe

Nathan clicked the link to download the attachment. Nervously, he glanced out his office window. Two tall gentlemen were walking down the OSP hallway toward his office. He placed them in their early 30s--one white, the other African-American. They moved effortlessly with the confidence that comes from power. Their toned figures made it obvious that they didn't work behind a desk all day.

Feds! He had to act fast. There was no time to look through the map of the Pentagon like he had planned. The computer script to the Pentagon's alarm system was now fully downloaded. He clicked "Run."

Immediately, loud sirens blared. Emergency lights flashed.

Nathan ran out of his office, taking a left to run away from the agents. Glancing over his shoulder, he saw the agents speeding up to follow him.

The other OSP employees attempted to make an orderly exit. Since 9/11, dozens of emergency evacuation drills had been run, and everyone had learned how to make a proper emergency exit.

"Mr. Alexander," one of the agents called out over the piercing alarm.

Nathan paid no attention to them. He quickened his pace, passing everyone.

"Mr. Alexander. We need a word with you."

Nathan weaved through the narrow hallway now cluttered with Pentagon personnel.

The agents lost all pretense of blending in as they yelled for people to get out of their way, shoving aside anyone in their path.

Nathan turned and now saw that only four Pentagon employees separated the agents from him. Nathan knew he'd never outrun them.

He ran toward the open corridor at end of the hallway where the escalators and stairwell were located. A security officer directed traffic to the stairwell in the corner of the corridor.

When Nathan reached the center of the corridor, he turned to face the agents toe-to-toe. The agents grabbed Nathan by the elbows and moved him out of the flow of traffic.

"Mr. Alexander," said the African-American agent. "We need a word with you."

"Who are you?" Nathan demanded.

"I'm Agent Malum with the FBI." Malum nodded to his colleague, "And this is my partner Andrew Stephens. We need to talk privately with you after we evacuate the building."

"FBI? Let me see your badge."

As the crowds of employees passed by to the stairwell, the agents took out their ID's. Nathan grabbed Malum's FBI badge and examined it, while Stephens held his ID in plain view.

As he examined the badge in his left hand, Nathan clenched his right fist. With all his strength, he sent his knuckles into agent Stephens' nose.

Before the agents could react, Nathan yanked his badge from his hands. He threw both badges in his pocket and ran toward the security officer at the stairwell.

Malum took out a gun, yelling at Nathan as he ran. "Stop right there!"

The busy room suddenly burst into high gear at the sight of the gun. The Pentagon employees rushed toward the stairwell, frantic to escape the potential gun fire.

Nathan froze. He kept his back to Malum and raised his hands overhead. He eyed the security officer at the stairwell. This was the same officer that greeted Nathan with a hearty "Good morning" everyday as walked to his office. "Officer, these men are responsible for setting off the alarm. They have no right to be here."

The security officer took out his pistol. He pointed the barrel at Malum and kept a close eye on Stephens.

"Officer, I'm Marcus Malum with the Federal Bureau of Investigation."

Stephens took his hand off his bloody nose long enough to talk. "Andrew Stephens...FBI."

"Check their badges," said Nathan. He inched toward the escalator to the lower floor.

Stephens now had one hand on his bloody nose and the other on his handgun. Malum kept his gun pointed at Nathan.

The security officer kept two hands on his weapon as he moved cautiously toward Malum. "Drop your weapon, and show me your documentation."

Malum turned his gun to point at the officer, one eye still on Nathan. "Our ID's are with him." Malum nodded in Nathan's direction. "They're in his right front pocket."

Nathan sprinted to the escalator.

"Stop him!" shouted Malum.

Stephens took off in pursuit.

The security officer pointed his gun at the moving Stephens. "Hold it, or I'll shoot!"

Stephens paid no attention to the security officer's demands as he chased after his target like a lion going after its prey.

The security official fired a shot, hitting Stephens in the lower calf. Stephens fell helplessly to the floor with blood pouring out above his Achilles heel.

Agent Malum ran up from behind the security officer and batted away his pistol. He grabbed the officer's lapels, nearly pulling him off his feet. "You idiot! We're on assignment to capture a Pentagon insider who's abating a terrorist." Malum reached into his pocket and jerked out a keycard. "Here's my access to FBI headquarters--is this good enough?"

While Stephens and Malum were convincing the security guard of their legitimacy, Nathan was making his way to the bottom of the escalator. Pentagon employees were instructed not to use the escalators in times of emergency, giving Nathan an open path to the first floor.

The first floor of Ring C was even more crowded than the narrow hallway upstairs. The area resembled a mall. Boutique stores and restaurants lined a wide walkway. Between the shops were doors that lead to other corridors and sectors. Throngs of employees were attempting to get to Ring E, the outermost ring of the complex. Nathan would have to fight through the herd to go in the other direction.

Malum helped his colleague back on his feet. Stephens wobbled on one leg, putting little weight on his right side.

"Go, go!" Stephens commanded. "Don't worry about me."

Malum raced to the escalator. When he got to the bottom, he scanned the room. He could not find Nathan within the flocks of people scattering to the exits. He fired two shots in the air. Everyone remained motionless. Malum looked into the distance and saw only one person moving--Nathan fighting his way upstream. Nathan turned, and the two made eye contact for a brief second.

Nathan ran faster, Malum in pursuit. Malum kept his gun in the air as the Pentagon employees made a path for him.

Nathan knew time was short. Almost two minutes had passed since he had sounded the alarm. Pentagon computers had a three-minute idle period before a password-protected screen would appear on the computer, preventing anyone besides the owner from using it. He only had a minute to get to one of the computers on Ring A or B. But first, he had to get Malum off his tail.

Nathan took notice of one of the doorways where people were flooding out. *The Navy. Perfect.* He was very familiar with this sector of the Pentagon. He'd spent his first years at the Pentagon in this sector.

He squeezed through the door and slammed the door shut behind him. He spread his arms out to stop the line of Naval officers trying to exit. "Attention Everyone! This door must remain shut. There's an overcrowding in the Ring C walkway. We must find an alternate route to Ring D. I REPEAT. THIS DOOR MUST REMAIN CLOSED."

Malum reached the door. He tried to open it but it was locked. He moved the door handle up and down with all his might, but the door would not open. He then saw there was a card reader and key pad next to the door. Malum stopped a man dressed in uniform in the walkway. "I need entry to this door. Can you swipe your ID for me?"

"My card won't work for that. Only the Navy guys have access to that sector."

Malum pounded his fist into the door.

Nathan took the shortest route possible to Ring B. To access Ring B, one needed a top-level security clearance. Luckily a security guard was holding the security gate open, letting a stream of employees funnel out.

Nathan ran past the officer, giving no reason for why he was entering. Nathan did not slow as he approached the line exiting out the door. He barreled through the line of employees, accidentally causing several in the line to topple over.

The officer took off in pursuit. However, by the time he climbed over the employees on the floor, Nathan had already entered into one of the dozens of hallways stemming from the corridor.

Nathan was now in a sector that had a long row of large offices. Nathan ran down the hallway until he spotted a glowing computer screen from the hall window. He tried opening the door to the office, but it was locked. Having no other options, he slammed his elbow into the center pane of the door and shattered the glass. *No need to worry about setting off any alarms.* He reached through the gaping hole to unlock it. Once inside, he jumped over the desk and moved the computer's mouse. He looked into the monitor. The three-minute-idle screen had yet to pop up.

Nathan clicked the mouse, moving from screen to screen as he searched for the computer's Network Access Code. After several minutes of searching, he found the 25-digit NAC. He took out the Blackberry and sent a text message to Daniel:

Got the code 1123581221091120011221973. Will try to get microfiche. But in trouble.

Chapter 24

Pentagon — File and Document Storage
September 19, 2006
9:10 a.m.

Nathan had made his way to the basement. No alarms were going off in this area. He was relieved to discover that nobody was down there.

Cautiously, he made his way to the file storage room and was surprised to see a security officer at the entrance. The officer was inside a glass room that looked like a movie theater's box office.

Nathan approached the glass and took out Agent Stephens' FBI identification, careful to keep his fingers over the picture. "Agent Stephens with the FBI. Why haven't you evacuated?"

"Not allowed," remarked the old, gray-haired officer. "Even if there were a nuclear bomb threat, I'd still be down here making sure no one tries to steal classified information." The officer set his coffee mug on the table in front of him. "What brings you down here?"

"We had a tip that someone has stolen documents. I'm searching for evidence to confirm or refute this. You'll need to open up."

The security officer leaned over and pushed a button. A large door to the storage room slowly started opening. "Need any help?"

"Where do you store the microfiche records and projector?"

The security officer pointed towards a specific aisle within the storage room. "All the way down and take a left."

Nathan surveyed the massive storage room--it was basically a warehouse filled with aisles of cabinets and files. He had to walk more than 300 feet just to reach the microfiche files.

On the first floor, Agent Malum had finally found his injured partner. They were making their way around the evacuated open-area walkway.

Malum felt his phone ring in his pocket. He took it out and saw "Wolf" on the caller ID. "Agent Malum."

"Markus, I'm calling to know your whereabouts."

"Agent Stephens and I are in one of the main corridors of the Pentagon. Our man went into a restricted sector. We were unable to follow."

"We've got him on video surveillance now. He's in the basement going through sensitive files. I need you two down there immediately."

"Yes, sir."

"And Markus--make sure he's alive. We need to know where he's getting his information."

Nathan held a microfiche sheet up to his eyes. It was a piece of film that was capable of holding over 100 microscopic images on one sheet. In his other hand was a file of fifty additional microfiche sheets recorded on November 22, 1998. He'd have to move fast to find what he was looking for.

Hurriedly, he placed the first sheet under the microfiche viewer. He briefly scanned the headlines of the documents on that sheet but found nothing having to do with "The Re Con."

His head snapped up as he heard footsteps echo from the entrance to the storage facility.

"That you?" he called out, hoping he'd hear the security guard reply.

Hearing nothing, he edged around the corner.

"Mr. Alexander, hold it right there!" Agent Malum's voice was firm and clear, even from all the way across the storage facility.

Nathan sprinted back to the microfiche projector. He grabbed the records he'd pulled. Desperately, he tried to find a place to hide.

Agent Malum signaled to his wounded partner. "Stay here, and make sure he doesn't try to escape. I'm going in after him." With gun in hand, he entered one of the rows of filing cabinets.

The storage room was a huge maze of files and shelves, some reaching nearly as high as the ceiling. Nathan tiptoed around the massive stacks, his heart throbbing in his ears. Malum rounded every corner with his gun ready.

"Mr. Alexander, I recommend you come out while you have a chance. I'm getting sick of chasing you around. It's of your best interest to turn yourself in before you get hurt. We both know you don't stand a chance."

Nathan froze. Malum's voice was close; the only thing separating them was an aisle of file cabinets. Malum had no idea Nathan was only a few feet on the other side.

Crouching, Nathan quietly put his shoulder and hands up to the wide metal cabinet. With one mighty push, he sent the large cabinet crashing down on top of Malum. Nathan ran for the exit while Malum was pinned down to the ground.

Upon hearing the clamor of the metal file, Stephens took out his two-way radio. "Markus, you need back up?"

He waited for several seconds. After hearing no response, he cautiously entered the storage room. Just then, an object flew his way, but he had no time to react. A 25-pound metal drawer from one of the filing cabinets slammed into his left shoulder, scattering papers and files everywhere. His injured leg was unable to support the blow. He fell to the floor, and Nathan ran past.

"Stop right there!" yelled the security officer from his glass office. It was too late--Nathan was already headed for the stairwell.

Nathan looked back and saw Stephens getting up on his one good leg. Stephens was the least of his worries. As long as Malum stayed down, he had a chance to escape.

The stairwell led Nathan to Ring C of a completely evacuated Pentagon. There were a few inspectors searching for the cause of the alarm, but they wouldn't give him any trouble.

Nathan ran down Ring's C main corridor to Ring D. By the time he reached the end, Nathan's adrenaline started to run low. He was starting to feel like a 44-year-old man again. His run slowed to a jog. *Come on--one more ring until I'm out of here.*

As Nathan approached the end of Ring E, bullets crashed into the wall beside him. Nathan turned and saw Malum at the end of the long corridor. He once again kicked it into high gear.

He barreled through the exit doors. There was nowhere to hide--the only thing in front of him was an empty parking lot where several of the evacuees had gathered. Considering Malum's physical shape, he knew that the federal agent could make up the 100-foot gap between them in a matter of seconds.

With no other alternative, Nathan darted into the parking lot with little hope that he'd reach his car before Malum caught him.

Nathan heard Malum burst through the exit doors. At the same time, he saw a car speeding toward him. *Trapped.* He stood frozen, like a deer caught in the headlights.

At the last second, the driver of the car slammed on brakes. The car screeched to a halt, stopping within a foot of Nathan's trembling body.

The window of the black sports car rolled down. "Hurry, get in!"

Chapter 25

Pentagon — Northwest Parking Lot
September 19, 2006
9:26 a.m.

Nathan had no time to think. He jumped into the car as Agent Malum closed in from behind.

"Hang on," a familiar voice called.

"Daniel!" shouted Nathan in relief.

Daniel put the accelerator to the floor and the car sped out of the lot. Malum fired a series of shots. One after another, three bullets hit the back window, splintering it beyond repair.

"Get down," yelled Daniel with his eyes on the road ahead of him. Nathan buried his head between his knees until the car was a sufficient distance from Malum.

Daniel watched as the agent disappeared in the rearview mirror. "How many more are in pursuit?"

"One," Nathan gasped for breath. "But we lost him…in the basement."

Daniel made a sharp turn onto a main highway. "You know who they were?"

"FBI," said Nathan, removing the badges from his pocket.

"Nice," said Daniel. "Those will come in handy." He peered at the manila file in Nathan's hand. "Are those the documents?"

Nathan sorted through the microfiche sheets. "Couldn't find the exact one--I just got them all. We'll need a microfiche reader."

"Won't be a problem," replied Daniel. "Any local library will have one."

Nathan took a minute to catch his breath. "You get the text message?"

"Yep, exactly what I was looking for."

Nathan looked back at the Pentagon as it faded into the distance. "How did you find me?"

Daniel reached into the backseat for his laptop. He handed it to Nathan. On the screen was a satellite image of the area around the Pentagon. A flashing red dot was going east down the highway.

Nathan pointed to the red dot. "Is this us?"

"That's you. I've been tracing your Blackberry."

Nathan took the large cell phone out of his pocket. "So this thing can be traced?"

"Oh yes, all mobile devices can. Fortunately, the government doesn't know that one belongs to you."

Nathan looked around the inside of the Pontiac GTO. "Where did you manage to find this?"

"There isn't anything you can't get on the black market, especially the black market here in D.C. You just have to be willing to give up some cash. That reminds me-- did you get the money?"

Nathan took out a key from his pocket. "It's all in a safety deposit box on the other side of town."

"We'll go get it later. It'd be wise to invest some of it in some firepower."

"I don't need any guns. I've got my dad's knife," replied Nathan wiping the sweat from his brow. "He started teaching me how to use it when I was seven. It's been awhile since I've seen real military action, but I'm as good at using it as any Navy Seal. Besides, you should've seen how I used a filing cabinet to take down the other FBI agent."

Daniel smiled. "I knew I chose the right man for the job."

Nathan looked out the window. "Where are we going?"

"Back to the warehouse to see if I can hack into the archived files using the NAC. But I think it'd be best if we split up for safety's sake. I suggest you go somewhere on the north side of town where there's not much video surveillance."

"Should I take the car?"

"No. The FBI agent has seen it--not to mention the bullet holes make it look a little suspicious. We'll trade it for another from the black market dealers."

"They'll do that?"

"Show'em enough money, and they can get you anything you want."

Chapter 26

205 F Street NE
September 20, 2006
8:25 p.m.

Nathan parked his new Ford Mustang in an empty parking lot. The black market dealer had also sold him a laptop and several other things he never realized someone could buy. He was now trying to give Daniel some time to do research at the warehouse.

While driving around town, he was able to find one of few telephone booths that still existed. He used it to make sure Claire was alright with staying with her grandmother. Daniel had warned him not make contact with anyone he knew, but Nathan figured that there was no harm in using a pay phone that couldn't be traced.

Nathan opened his new laptop that had global wireless Internet access. He connected to *Scholars for 9/11 Truth & Justice*, a website run by college professors and professionals who had conducted extensive research on 9/11.

The *Scholars'* research focused mainly on the 9/11 events in New York City. They had little evidence concerning the Pentagon. Nathan knew that if he and Daniel could combine their inside information with the *Scholars'* evidence, they'd have a powerful platform that would be heard. He wrote down three names from the group he believed could help: Stephen E. Jones, Jim Hoffman, and Bob Bowman.

Nathan continued to read the Scholars for 9/11 Truth & Justice website until his Blackberry mobile device notified him that he had received a text message. Nathan opened the message.

Just went thru the archived files. Incredible. Meet me at our spot 2nite. D L

Chapter 27

```
1227 Ridgeway Ave.
September 20, 2006
         9:11 p.m.
```

Nathan squeaked open the warehouse's metal door and stepped into the darkness behind it. In the far corner, Daniel worked under the faint glow of his laptop screen.

Nathan slowly walked towards him, carefully stepping over crates and stacks of old documents. "So the NAC code was helpful? What all have you found?"

"More than I thought. I found some more information about government involvement in 9/11." Daniel turned the computer screen so that it faced Nathan. "Then I found what I was looking for…"

Out of nowhere, the sound of two gunshots filled the room. The first hit the computer screen and everything went black. Nathan then heard Daniel fall to the floor.

"Daniel!"

Silence.

Nathan reached down to the ground and grabbed Daniel's chest. "Aaaaaaah!" Nathan jerked back his hand when he felt the warm liquid. Daniel's blood dripped from his fingertips.

Realizing he was next in line, he rolled across the floor to take cover behind a stack of wooden crates.

He put his back up to one of the crates, squeezed his eyes shut, and tilted his head to the ceiling. He was breathing so deep, anyone in the room could hear his distress. He was in a state of shock. He tried to make sense of what he should do-- but his brain could only concentrate on that fact that Daniel was lying a few feet away in a puddle of blood.

Suddenly, a hand reached out and grabbed his wrist.

Chapter 28

1227 Ridgeway Ave.
September 20, 2006
9:13 p.m.

Nathan opened his eyes, attempting to identify the man who would claim his life.

He then realized it was Daniel's bloody hand around his wrist.

"They found us," Nathan moaned hopelessly.

"Listen to me," said Daniel, trying to keep upright on his knees. "Behind you is a black crate." Daniel coughed. The bullet in his lung was causing blood to erupt from his mouth. "Under it..." he paused and coughed again, "is a tunnel. Take it. It's your only chance."

"What's the point?"

Daniel's cold hand turned Nathan's wrist so that his palm was facing up. He grabbed a pen from his pocket and pressed it into Nathan's palm. He guided the pen across Nathan's hand.

Nathan could feel Daniel losing strength as the pen lost its firmness against his skin. Daniel wrote one last letter and collapsed.

Nathan then heard the unmistakable tread of footsteps moving through the darkness. Desperately, he turned to the crate behind him and pushed it back to reveal a manhole. He dove head-first into the hole, then twisted his body around to pull the crate back in place.

Nathan had no idea what was around him. All he could feel was dirt. He used his hands to pull himself forward as he crawled on his belly through the blackness.

After a few minutes of crawling, he reached a narrow point in the tunnel. Movement was impossible. *Daniel was skinner than me.* Just then, something hairy whisked across his nose. *A rat!!!*

Nathan did not know what was going to kill him first--the assassins in the warehouse or the disease-infested rats in the tunnel.

He kicked, shook, and squirmed to break free. The stagnant air was hard to breath. Rats crawled down his back, their claws raking his skin. Fear alone propelled him to keep trying to go forward. Finally, he felt something give way. He crawled on his elbows and knees squirming even faster through the tight passage.

Nathan continued down the passageway until he ran into a dead end. He felt overhead. Nothing there. Arching his back, he stood up. He raised his hands overhead and pushed back a large piece of cardboard. He pulled himself up onto the surface. He frantically patted down his body, ridding himself of rodents and dirt.

In the distance he saw the Hampton Inn Hotel. He was in the same alleyway as the warehouse, just a little further down.

Instead of going back in the direction from which he came, Nathan headed to the other end of the alley. He was fully aware a sniper might be aiming at him that very second. He didn't know whether to run or to walk quietly. Hoping for the best, Nathan quietly attempted a circular route back to his car.

Nathan had the strange feeling that this dark alley symbolized his future. He had nowhere to go. Nowhere to turn. He had lost everything. All he had was enough information for someone to want him dead.

Chapter 29

3000 Ridgeway Ave.
September 20, 2006
9:22 p.m.

At the opposite end of the alley, Nathan found a well-lit street crowded with apartments and office buildings. As soon as he rounded the corner, Nathan quickened his pace. He had to get back to his car before the assassins figured out he had escaped through the tunnel. He hadn't heard anybody exit the warehouse behind him, but he knew government agents were probably in the vicinity. Unfortunately, his car was another two blocks away--he had listened to Daniel's advice about parking in a lot that had no video surveillance

Nathan wondered if the bullet that hit the laptop was aimed at him. *The irony is that Daniel's laptop was probably more valuable than my life.* It was then that Nathan realized the magnitude of what just happened. Without Daniel, he did not have the research to disprove the official 9/11 story.

As he continued down the sidewalk, Nathan ran into a woman coming down the stairs to her apartment.

"Watch it!" yelled the woman, as she tripped and went down on one knee.

Nathan instinctively reached down to help her up. When she saw his blood stained hand, she let out a high-pitch shrill that echoed into the night.

There was no time to be a gentleman--Nathan had to get back to his car before the shooters could find out where the scream had come from.

Nathan sprinted down the city street, not even slowing down to look back.

When he reached his car, he had no idea on where he should go. He just knew that he needed to get out of Washington D.C. He cranked up the car and started driving.

As he made a sharp left turn onto the highway, Nathan looked down at his hand. He opened his palm and turned on the car's interior light. Daniel's dying message stared him straight in the face. Eight numbers--10221963. *What could it mean?*

Chapter 30

Aberdeen, Maryland
September 20, 2006
11:35 p.m.

Nathan drove northeast on I-95. Being thirty miles outside of Baltimore, he felt he was far enough outside Washington to safely stop for fuel.

Nathan stared numbly at the eight numbers on his hand-- they were barely readable. Not only had sweat from his hand smudged the ink, but Daniel's writing was not all that clear in the first place.

He could not think of anything that had an eight-number sequence. Nathan recalled how quickly Daniel was losing strength when he was writing. *Maybe there were more numbers that Daniel was unable to write. If it were nine numbers, it could be a Social Security number.*

He pulled into the nearest gas station and took out his laptop. He wanted to see if he could find certain Social Security numbers on the Internet. To his surprise, he found a website which allowed anyone to look up someone's ten-year history just by entering their Social Security Number into a provided search engine. It was supposed to be used for employer background checks, but Nathan used it to his advantage.

He typed in the first eight digits, then added numbers *0-9* one by one in the place of the last digit. However, none of these ten Social Security number searches came back with a living person.

Thinking it might be a nine-digit ZIP code, he visited the Google Maps website and entered the numbers into its search engine. The result was Columbia, MD. Nathan had just driven through Columbia. This was a huge coincidence, but he was sure that there was nothing in this small town of any interest.

Nathan looked at his computer, trying to think of a solution. *What about an IP address?* An IP address is the unique number sequence assigned to computers and websites. *Daniel was a computer guy. It'd make sense if it had something to do with the Internet.*

Nathan quickly researched IP addresses, then tried putting the eight numbers in every possible combination. Once again, no solutions came back for the IP addresses he tried.

Nathan was stumped. He decided to check his Gmail account to see if Daniel had sent him anything before they had met that evening.

Nathan typed in his username, *T.Ruth.Moore@gmail.com*, then entered his password: *911Truth.*

Nathan paused before pressing enter. "911Truth," he said out loud. *An eight-letter password-- that's it!*

Nathan pulled up the boc.ix email account. He entered Daniel's username, *DL*, then entered the password: *10221963*. He pressed enter, and it gave him access to the account.

Nathan's eyes grew wide.

Daniel's account was full of hundreds of emails, all of which he had sent to himself, except for the few Nathan had sent. Nathan opened one of the emails.

Subject: The Neocon Document
From: DL@boc.ix
To: DL@boc.ix
Date: 4/13/04

The PNAC's 2000 report: Rebuilding America's Defenses: Strategies, Forces, And Resources For A New Century.

Attachment: RebuildingAmerica'sDefenses.tif

Nathan downloaded the attached file and discovered it was a scanned image of the infamous PNAC report. Daniel had highlighted all the controversial portions with a yellow highlighter pen.

Nathan opened another.

Subject: More Stuff on the Neocons
From: DL@boc.ix
To: DL@boc.ix
Date: 4/13/04

PNAC is not the only group who is a part of the military-industrial complex in America. PNAC planned 9/11, but these groups have also been involved in corrupt politics that are helping to establish the New World Order:

* *RAND*
* *AEI*
* *CFR*
* *The Illuminati*
* *Trilateral Commission*

Of these five groups, the Trilateral Commission is the most influential. The 350 individuals in the Tri Com are some of the most powerful people in the world. The members of the upper elite are using their power to control the masses.

It's not surprising that many of the Tri Com's members had a hand in 9/11:

•Paul Wolfowitz (one of PNAC's top guys, Bush Doctrine, President of World Bank)
•Dick Cheney (PNAC, vice-president)
•George H.W. Bush (Former President)
•Henry Kissinger (neocon who was first selected to head the 9/11 commission; former National Security Advisor)

- *Z. Brzezinski (neocon author of The Grand Chessboard – a book similar to PNAC's Rebuilding America's Defenses; former National Security Advisor)*
- *Frank Carlucci (President of Carlyle Group; member of PNAC and RAND)*

Attachment:
CompleteTriComList.dat, PossibleNWOconspirators.doc

Nathan looked through the rest of the emails. All of them had attachments containing pictures, documents, and other evidence concerning the cover-up of 9/11. *Daniel must've been using his email account as back-up storage for all his research.* Nathan then realized that he all needed to disprove 9/11 was in front of him.

A car door slammed, and Nathan nearly jumped out of his seat. He looked up to see the man in the car next to him reach for the nozzle at the gas pump. This reminded him of why he stopped in the first place.

He filled up his car and went inside to pay. As he walked back to his car, Nathan tried to think of a place where he could sort through Daniel's research. He needed to find a secure location. He needed to find someone who could help get this information out to the world.

There was only one person he could completely trust. Only one person who wouldn't think he had lost his mind. He cranked up his car and headed in that direction.

Chapter 31

New Haven, Connecticut
September 21, 2006
6:15 p.m.

Nathan knocked on the door of the second floor apartment. Moments later, his 19-year-old son opened the door.

"Dad, what are you doing here?" asked Nick as he held the door open. He quickly moved towards the living room as Nathan came in. Nick picked up dirty clothes, old pizza boxes, and the mess around the living room. "I was just cleaning up," said Nick, frantically trying to get everything in order.

"Don't worry about it," Nathan showed no concern about the mess. It actually reminded him what it was like to be in college. "I'm not here to check up on you." Nathan looked down at the dirt on his clothes from the tunnel. "Besides, look at the mess on me."

"Why are you here? And why do you look so nasty?" Nick sniffed. "And smelly?"

Nathan looked at Nick's roommate who was watching TV on the sofa. His attention was now on them. "Is there somewhere private we can go?"

"Sure, we can go to my bedroom."

Nathan and Nick walked into one of the bedrooms adjacent to the living room. Nick shut the door behind him. "Dad, is everything okay? Claire called me a couple days ago. She was worried about you."

Nathan took a deep breath. He took the next hour explaining how he was now holding the information that could change America's history.

Nathan looked into his son's eyes, "Do you believe me?"

"Of course I do."

"You don't think the idea of the government carrying out 9/11 is too far-fetched?"

Nick stood to face Nathan. At 5'10" he was just a bit shorter than his father. "I've been trying to tell you this for years. Since coming to Yale, I've even joined a '9/11 Cover-up' group on Facebook."

Nathan had a puzzled look on his face. "Facebook?"

Taking into consideration the seriousness of the situation, Nick refrained from rolling his eyes and giving his dad the "*Are you really that old?*" look. "Facebook.com is a website that college students use to interact with each other. You're connected to other people through friends, schools, and groups. One of the groups I've joined is a political group who wants the truth about 9/11. And it's not just liberal college students in the group--there are a lot of professors and even a couple politicians involved."

"Why didn't you ever tell me about this?"

"Dad, you work for the government. Why would I tell you I support a group that opposes what your reports say? That'd be like the son of Marlboro's CEO telling his dad that he contributed money to an anti-smoking campaign."

"I see your point," said Nathan. "So, you'll help me?"

"Of course. What kind of son wouldn't help out his dad who's running for his life because he wants to do the right thing?"

"Great, because I'm going to need all the help I can get." Nathan paused and looked around the bedroom. "I'm also going to need a place to stay. I don't want to put you at risk by getting you involved, but right now I see no other option."

"No, I'd love for you to stay here." Nick opened the door and looked into his living room. "The living room is pretty messy, but you're welcome to sleep on the sofa."

"What about your roommate?"

"Jay's cool. He won't mind."

"Still, I'd like to be somewhere more private. I want to do some research on my laptop and not have to worry about someone finding out that I'm here."

Nick walked over to his closet. "I got a fairly big walk-in closet."

Nathan looked in the closet. "This might just work. It's long enough for me lie down and sleep. It has an electrical outlet to charge up my laptop. And during the day, I could shut the door and have a quiet workplace." Nathan took a seat on the carpeted floor. "I'll just stay in here."

"Sweet, my dad will be staying in my closet," Nick thought aloud. "I'm sure all the girls on campus will be dying to stay at my place for the night."

"Girls?"

"Dad, I'm joking. I'm excited that you're here and what you're trying to do. For the last couple years I've desperately wanted to convince you about 9/11. Now that we're seeing eye-to-eye, I'll gladly take the sacrifices to help in whatever way I can."

Chapter 32

New Haven, Connecticut—Millard Stations
Apartments
September 22, 2006
12:57 a.m.

Nick opened the door of the closet, waking up his father. "Dad, I need to show you something."

Nathan rubbed his eyes and looked at his watch. "It's one o'clock in the morning. Not to mention I've been up for the last thirty-six hours."

Nathan followed his son into the living room where three college students rose to greet him. Nathan's half-closed eyes grew wide. Without acknowledging them, he turned and went back into Nick's room. Nick followed his father into the bedroom.

"Relax. They're some of my friends. I told them your story. They're here to help."

Nathan tried to keep his voice to a whisper, but it bore tones of alarm. "Nick, nobody's supposed to know about me being here."

"Whatever happened to 'I could use all the help I can get'? Don't worry, they aren't undercover FBI agents. Let me introduce them to you."

Reluctantly, Nathan followed Nick back into the living room. "Guys, this is my dad."

Nick pointed to a tall, skinny young man wearing thin-framed glasses. "This is Hunt Sexton. He's a pre-law guy who's also on Facebook's '9/11 Cover-up' with me. He's involved with a bunch of political activities that's trying to restore our Constitutional rights."

Nick pointed to a young red-haired man on the sofa. "And of course you know my roommate, Jay. He's actually the one who first told me about the Truth Movement."

Nick then nodded toward the short, bearded young man in the corner. "And this is Joseph Duke. He's not heavily involved in the 9/11 Truth Movement, but he's really concerned about America and current politics. He actually thinks that America is on the verge of entering a state of fascism like Nazi Germany."

Nathan smiled cautiously. "Guys, I thank you for your willingness to help, but we're talking about serious stuff. I don't want to endanger your lives by bringing any of you into this. It'd be best that you don't know what's going on."

"But we already know what's going on in our government," said Hunt. "It's a bunch of shit. And as an American, I'm not going to stand for it. I'll gladly risk my life to be a patriot like Samuel Adams."

"You see, Mr. Alexander, we plan to live in this country for at least another sixty years," said Jay. "We'll do anything to prevent the rise of a tyrannical government that lies to us and takes us into wars we don't want to fight."

"We're talking about the truth, exposing corruption, our nation's future," said Nick. "There's no way we're backing down. Not now. Not ever. We're in this together, Dad."

Nathan was awestruck. "I can't thank you guys enough for your passion and commitment. If you guys are able to show the same determination and energy when my report comes out, I don't think we'll have any problem telling every American about the truth."

"What report?" asked Nick.

"I'm going to write a formal report--writing it in the fashion that I'd write a government report for the Pentagon. Seeing how many resources I have on my computer, this report will probably be over 500 pages. I also want to create a brief article or video--something that every American could read or watch to get the gist of what really happened on 9/11."

Nick spoke up. "I could help you with this. You know how much I like to research and write. And Jay's pretty good with cameras and technology."

"Good, I'll share with you the main points and sources that should be highlighted. Also, I'm going to need a lot of additional research. The libraries on campus should have all I need--they have Internet access, printers, databases, not to mention millions of books and newspapers. You guys think you could get me access into them?"

Joseph yanked out a driver's license from his wallet. "Since I turned 16, I've had an ID saying I'm 21. Getting a fake ID won't be a problem. I actually work in the library."

"Good. Any volunteers to help with the research?"

All four nodded. "Oh yeah."

"Dad, this is much bigger than anything else in our lives--we're talking about a huge turning point in American history. We'll be glad to help in any way we can."

Nathan felt good about having four energetic college kids helping him out. With their assistance, he was confident that he could deliver a report to the media in one month's time. He knew it would not be easy. He'd have to shave his head and grow a beard to mask his identity in case the Pentagon put out a search for him. He'd also have to work at a rapid pace while keeping an eye out for anyone who could be watching him. On the positive side, however, he had plenty of savings to live on, a secure place to hide, and access to mountains of information. Nick could even call Claire to tell her that Nathan had been assigned to an urgent month-long assignment. With any luck, he could pull this off.

He was too excited after their conversation to go back to bed just yet. He decided to look over Daniel's emails a little more. He sat down on a beanbag in the closet and opened the boc.ix account.

He sorted Daniel's emails by "most recent" and discovered that Daniel had written three just before he died. Nathan opened the first one.

Subject: The 9/11 of the 20th century
From: DL@boc.ix
To: DL@boc.ix
Date: 9/20/06

I never thought I'd come across this in the archived files – it seems as though Lee Harvey Oswald was not the only one involved in the plot to kill President John F. Kennedy.
Attachment: JFKassassination.doc

Nathan opened the attachment and saw it was a list of several dozen names, many of whom were key figures in politics during the 60s.

Interesting. The JFK assassination was a little bit before Nathan's time, but he knew that there was a wave of controversy surrounding it. He knew Daniel's list of names was far from providing substantial proof that government figures were involved in a conspiratorial plot, but he felt this information could be very helpful in the future.

Nathan opened the second email to see if it could shed some light more light on the first.

Subject: Where the Secret Lies
From: DL@boc.ix
To: DL@boc.ix
Date: 9/20/06

The secret lies within Harvard and Yale.
The Government School + Skull & Bones

Nathan looked at the first line. *At Yale? Now what does this mean? Maybe it will help to look at this in the morning when my mind is fresh.*

Before going to bed, Nathan had to take a quick look at the third email.

Subject: The Top Secret Information
From: DL@boc.ix
To: DL@boc.ix
Date: 9/20/06

Who would've guessed the top secret information I was looking for is actually secrets of secret societies. What's the most shocking part is that these groups have always been in politics and positions of power.

Attachment: TheSecret.dat

Without opening the file, Nathan knew exactly what "The Secret" referred to.

He took a moment to reflect. *It's 2:30 in the morning, and I'm sitting on a bean bag in my son's closet reading about how conspiracies have changed this world's history. Am I dreaming?*

Chapter 33

Millard Station Apartments
September 22, 2006
7:07 a.m.

Nathan woke up before he could get a full night's rest; he was eager to do some more research. He wanted to know exactly what the fourth reason behind 9/11 was—the reason that Daniel was referring to as "The Secret."

Nathan reexamined the second email: "The Secret lies at Harvard and Yale." *Daniel must've known of a source at these two campuses that could provide valid proof.* Nathan knew of one possibility. He was ready to search the Yale campus to see what he could find, but Nick's friend had yet to bring him a fake ID.

Doing nothing was unbearable to someone addicted to work like he was, so he began an Internet search on Harvard to see what "secrets" may be associated with the school. As he searched, he recalled something Daniel had told him about Harvard and Yale two weeks before:

"The neoconservative movement started gaining popularity in the '60s just before Kennedy was assassinated. After retiring from political office, this first generation of neocons became professors at Ivy League Schools--HARVARD and YALE. These first-generation neocons taught their neoconservative beliefs to George

W. Bush and the PNAC guys."

Nathan began to realize the implications. *These schools are centers for the neocon movement. But what else? What secrets are they hiding?*

Within the second e-mail, Nathan knew exactly what "Skull & Bones" meant, but he had no clue on what Daniel was referring to by "The Government School." He typed the phrase into the search area on Harvard's website. Nathan was taken aback when the results appeared.

The name of Harvard's government school was the John F. Kennedy School of Government. Daniel hinted that the neocons were involved in assassinating Kennedy--Nathan wondered if the name of the school was brought forth by the neocons who carried a sense of pride in how they got rid of Kennedy. Nathan realized that this idea was a stretch, so he did not think too much of it until he saw the school's logo:

Veritas, he whispered. The Latin word for truth. He stared at the image. A shield of veritas--or, in other words, "protectors of the truth" or "shielding the truth." *This definitely reflects Daniel's idea of Harvard being an institution that's keeping secrets.*

Nathan clicked though Harvard's website until another glaring point caught his eye. Harvard's Dean of Defense Studies during Kennedy's assassination was Henry Kissinger. Nathan recalled seeing Kissinger's name on Daniel's list of those involved in plotting JFK's murder. *I'm sure Kissinger was the one who brought forth the idea of changing the name of the school to the "John F. Kennedy Government School."*

Nathan knew that Kissinger was a heavily-criticized politician whose pro-war beliefs probably fell in the lines of being neoconservative. After Kennedy's assassination, Kissinger was eventually promoted by his friends in Washington to be the Secretary of State.

Nathan clicked a link to take him to Kissinger. As he read his biography, his stomach started to feel at unease. President Bush had first chosen Kissinger to head the 9/11 Commission Report--the so-called "investigation" of 9/11. *No wonder Bush wanted Kissinger to be in charge of the Commission--he's a neocon who would've been glad to cover up the facts, just like he did for JFK's assassination.*

All these neocon connections were certainly more than mere coincidence.

Chapter 34

Millard Stations Apartments
September 22, 2006
4:10 p.m.

Later that afternoon, Nick knocked on his closet's door. "Dad, we got you a school ID."

Nathan unlocked the door to the closet and met his son and his friends in the living room.

Joseph handed Nathan the card. "This should give you access to the libraries and most other buildings on campus."

"Great. I need to go to the library to research. I wish I could visit Harvard's campus, but hopefully I'll find all I need here at Yale. By the way, do you guys know about the Skull and Bones secret society here at Yale?

Nick patted Jay on the shoulder. "Jay's hoping he'll get 'tapped' into the society so he can become a member next year."

"What political science major wouldn't?" said Jay. "It's a given that Bonesmen have an incredible amount of success."

Joseph looked at Jay. "What exactly are Bonesmen?"

"That's just the name of those in Skull and Bones. You know, the group that meets in the 'Bones Tomb' building next to Hunt's place."

"I can sometimes hear them late at night," said Hunt. "It's a lot of weird sounds--I have no clue what they're doing."

"Nobody does--that's why it's a 'secret' society. Even after they graduate, the 15 members from each year's class vow that they won't tell anyone about the society. But from what I hear, Bonesmen do some pretty outrageous things."

Nick looked to his father. "Why did ya want to know about them?"

"They may have something I need. That reminds me--there's something else I need. Nick, do you have a subscription to Netflix?"

"Who doesn't?"

"Could you see if it has a documentary called *JFK II--The Bush Connection*?"

"Why do you want see that?"

"I don't think it has anything to do 9/11, but I'd like to learn something about the JFK assassination. I read a statistic that said 75% of Americans believe that government was somehow involved in assassinating JFK. By relating 9/11 to another well-known government conspiracy, I may be able to add some credibility to my report."

Jay opened his laptop and typed the title of the film into his computer. "You don't have to get it from Netflix. You can watch it for free on Google Video."

"Right now?"

Jay slid his laptop to face Nathan. All five of them crowded around the computer and watched the 90-minute documentary.

The movie provided overwhelming evidence that the JFK assassination was conceived and carried out by top government leaders. George H.W. Bush was supposedly one of the main figures involved. Others accused of being in the plot in the film were also on Daniel's list.

The five of them were completely dumbfounded by the evidence. After watching the thought-provoking film, all five of them realized that the 41st president was involved in dirty politics in the JFK affair, just like George W. Bush with 9/11.

Jay shook his head in disbelief. "It's amazing what some men will do to get more power."

"They'll certainly hide the truth," said Nathan as she stood up from the sofa. "I've seen this over and over again as I've gone through Daniel's research. I even found subtle meanings within Harvard University's logos that symbolize hiding the truth."

"Have you seen the logo for Yale's School of Management?" Jay asked.

"What about it?"

"We just had an article about it in the school paper." Nick went over to a stack of newspapers and magazines in the corner. "I may still have that copy."

Jay took out a dollar bill from his pocket and continued. "The logo's basically a shield with the motto 'Novus Ordo Seclorum' written on it."

Novus Ordo Seclorum, said Nathan, thinking aloud. "That actually sounds vaguely familiar."

Jay handed Nathan the dollar bill that he was reading from. "It's on the back of the dollar--right below the pyramid and ever-present eye."

"What does this phrase mean?"

Nick came back with a campus newspaper in his hand. "It says here that it translates to 'New Order of the Ages'."

"Or loosely translated, 'New World Order'," added Jay.

Daniel's warnings about the NWO flooded Nathan's mind. "New World Order? That's the motto?"

Nick placed the paper down on the coffee table and pointed to the upper portion of the shield that displayed an open book. "And above it is a book with a Hebrew inscription. Guess what it says?"

"What?"

"Light and truth."

"*Truth*--seems to be a recurring theme." Nathan paused to think of the significance of the metaphors conveyed by the image. "I'm maybe looking into this too much--but does this image look like it's conveying a hidden message?"

"I definitely think there's a deeper meaning behind it," said Jay. "I mean, why would a business school choose 'New World Order' as its motto?"

"Could you say it represents the school's desire to educate business leaders of the New World Order?" asked Joseph.

"I doubt that's true," said Hunt with slight skepticism. "But it does make for an interesting story. Dan Brown could write another *Da Vinci Code*-like novel about all this hidden meanings and conspiracy stuff."

Nathan smiled. "Unfortunately, we're not writing a novel--we're trying to tell the world the truth about 9/11. But if I'm reading Daniel's emails right, the ones who plotted 9/11 have this New World Order mindset. In fact, I believe there's a group with this mindset here at Yale that probably has inside information on 9/11. It may be worth a trip to the library to look into."

Chapter 35

Yale University Library
September 22, 2006
6:05 p.m.

Before walking over to the library, Nathan removed his father's Navy SEAL knife from his pocket. "I probably shouldn't carry this with me. The Pentagon hasn't put out any searches yet, but still, I don't want to take any chances of causing suspicion." He handed the family heirloom to his son. "You still remember the self-defense moves I taught you?"

Nick took the blade out from the protective case and whisked it around. "You bet." Nick started to combine martial arts moves with his knife swings. "Plus, I'm still pretty good at all the self defense moves I learned from five years of Karate."

"Hopefully, you'll never have to use those moves. But now, I'm actually glad I paid over $5,000 in Karate lessons to get you all the way to a black belt."

With his phony ID, Nathan had no trouble getting onto the library's computers. There, he searched the Internet to see what he could find about Skull and Bones. A quick visit to an online encyclopedia told him that the group was a secret society that offered membership to 15 Yale seniors every year. As Nick's friends had already revealed, almost every Yale student wanted to be in this exclusive group because Bonesmen were guaranteed a career of power and wealth after they graduated.

Nathan searched through many Yale databases hoping to find more information. He was able to pull up a complete list of Bonesmen that dated back to 1900. Nathan could not believe the number of famous people on the list. Two of the names stuck out--George W. Bush and George H.W. Bush.

Other names on the list included: John Kerry (the Democratic 2004 presidential candidate), William Taft (27th President), Henry Luce (founder of *Time Magazine*), David McCullough (best-selling biographer of politicians), several Rockefellers (business conglomerates and politicians), numerous CIA members, and too many elected politicians to count.

Almost every name on the list had become either a big-time player in Washington or a CEO for a large corporation. Skull and Bones was no average college organization. In fact, some called the group a "political mafia" that would do whatever it took to get its members to power.

Nathan continued to scroll down the list of members. One caught his eye: W. Averell Harriman, a confidant to President John F. Kennedy. *A confidant? This means Harriman was close enough to JFK that they met frequently to discuss confidential information.*

Nathan visited *Wikipedia* to find more about Harriman. He discovered that Harriman's good friend and fellow Bonesman was Prescott Bush, the father of George H. W. Bush. But Harriman's connection to the Bush family did not stop there. Harriman gave George H.W. Bush and Prescott Bush lucrative jobs at his bank during the 1930s. The FBI eventually shut down this bank for cooperating with Nazis during World War II.

Nathan went back to Daniel's list and found Harriman's name among those who were more than likely involved in JFK's assassination.

As he scrolled down the webpage, he found another interesting name on the Skull & Bones list--William Henry Donaldson. Donaldson founded the Yale School of Management in 1976, and was probably the one who made sure "New World Order" was prominently displayed on school's logo.

Nathan then did a quick search on George W. Bush's connections with Skull and Bones. At this point, Nathan was not surprised when the glaring results appeared. Bush had appointed at least five other Bonesmen to be a part of his administration. *Isn't it ironic how members of Skull and Bones seem to be connected to the two major events that have transformed American policy in the last half century? No wonder people refer to Skull and Bones as the 'political mafia.' Members of this mafia, however, don't spend time in jail--they spend time in Congress and the Oval Office.*

Before leaving, Nathan found a comprehensive book in the library that explained Skull and Bones and the many controversies surrounding the society. Even the conservative author of this book took an entire chapter to describe the conspiratorial claims of the group being nothing but a group of power-hungry individuals who want to use their influence to establish a "New World Order."

On his way out, an unsettling thought hit Nathan. *Maybe 9/11 isn't just a government conspiracy--but it's a small part of a conspiracy on a much greater scale.*

Nathan returned to the apartment, where Nick and Hunt were doing research on false flag terrorism.

"I need to get into the Bones Tomb," Nathan stated bluntly as the door closed behind him.

Nick gave his father a puzzled look. "You need what?"

"I pretty sure there's something there that would prove some of their past members were involved in corrupt politics."

"So what are you thinking?" asked Nick. "Break into Skull and Bones' house?"

"Unless they're now offering tours," said Nathan lightly. "According to the books in the library, they keep the door triple-locked."

"It wouldn't matter that it's tripled-locked," responded Hunt. "I could get you in using one key."

"How?"

"Since the Bones Tomb is on the Yale Campus, Yale police and administration must be able to access it. The campus police have a universal key that unlocks all old-fashioned locks on campus."

"And?"

"My friend actually has one of these keys. He left his backpack in the biology lab one night and needed to get it to study for a test the next day. He asked the police if they could let him in, but since they were busy with other things, they let him borrow the universal key if he promised to bring it right back. He figured that having one of these keys would be pretty useful if he ever wanted to play a prank, so he went to Wal-Mart and had a duplicate made really quick."

"You think you could get this key for us?"

"Just tell me when."

"When would be the best time to sneak in?"

"Obviously after dark," said Nick.

"What's today? Friday?" asked Hunt, thinking aloud. "We could go tonight. They only meet there twice a week-- on Tuesdays and Thursdays."

"Tonight is perfect," said Nathan.

Chapter 36

The Bones Tomb
September 22, 2006
11:45 p.m.

Hunt, Nick, and Nathan stood outside the mysterious Greco-Roman mansion that had been nicknamed "The Bones Tomb."

As Nathan unlocked the triple deadbolt, Nick stared at the eerie, cold building. The boxy gray structure only had a couple of windows--they obviously didn't want anybody to know what happened inside. It was also covered in symbols and signs associated with the occult. Above the iron door was an image of an Egyptian pyramid and the ever-present eye found on the back of a U.S. dollar bill. *Novus Ordo Seclorum*, he whispered under his breath.

Nathan quietly opened the door. All three of them immediately turned on their flashlights and looked around. The entire interior was decorated with skulls and bones--not your normal Halloween decoration, but real human bones. Fake coffins and gravestones were scattered about.

"This place is sick," said Nick as he glanced around the room that was exuding a sense of death.

Nathan shined his flashlight into a glass case that faced the front door. Inside the case were shelves that held the Skull and Bones most prized possessions. Nathan pointed to a set of forks and knives. "See that silverware?"

Nick shined his light in that direction.

"It belonged to the Nazis. Hitler himself supposedly used that very set." Nathan pointed his flashlight to a human skull within the glass case. "You know who that is?"

"Who?"

"Geronimo, the Native American. Bush's grandfather, Prescott Bush, dug into sacred ground just so they could add this famous skull to the Bones' collection. They're so proud of it that they've had it displayed here since 1918."

Nathan walked through the foyer into the main room--it was a large open room with a big dining room table in the center. The table was large enough to seat 25 people; the entire room was large enough to accommodate fifty people.

Nick pointed his flashlight toward a wood coffin that sat atop the large table. "What are we looking for?"

"Not sure. Just keep your eyes peeled."

"We're just hoping to stumble across something that has to do with 9/11?"

"No, according to the book, there should be a reading room that connects to this one." Nathan pointed his flashlight to the left corner and spotted a door. "There it is."

They entered the reading room and discovered it was a small library with a fireplace and several comfortable leather seats. Shelves of books reached the ceiling.

Nathan hurriedly scanned the titles of the thousands of books housed in the room. Most of them had been penned by Bonesmen who had once studied in that same room.

Nick and Hunt made their way to a closet in the corner. Hunt opened the door as Nick looked over his shoulder.

"Anything in there?" asked Nathan.

Hunt stuck his head in the dusty closet. "Nothing but coats and umbrellas."

Nathan studied the layout of the room and walked over to the closet. "Wait a second..." Nathan spread the coats on the coat hangers and uncovered a door behind them. "It only makes sense that a secret society would have a secret room."

Nathan opened the four-foot door. The secret room was just large enough for all three of them to enter. Stacked in the room were books, symbols, costumes, and other random items--it resembled an unorganized attic.

Nathan scanned the room until he saw a small ornate treasure chest. He shined his light upon it. "The Bones Box," he said, placing his hands on the chest. "Supposedly, it holds their most valuable treasure." He moved everything out of the way to get to it. He struggled to pick up the small, but heavy chest.

"That thing looks like it was used by actual pirates," said Nick.

"The chest itself is probably worth a fortune." Hunt glided his hand on the brass on the outside. "No telling what's inside."

Nathan tried opening it, but couldn't get it to budge.

As they pondered ways to open the chest, Nathan heard something. "Do you hear that?" he whispered.

"What?" Hunt whispered back.

The three of them froze as they heard footsteps coming from the direction of the main room.

Nathan motioned for the other two to wait in the secret room as he silently made his way back into the reading room.

He positioned himself carefully where he could see into the main room without being seen himself. He watched as a total of 15 students walked in--13 male students wearing coats and ties and two females wearing formal dresses.

The small torches they carried kept the room fairly dark. After placing their torches in their holsters, they took a seat around the large table in the center. None of them said a word.

Hunt and Nick crept up behind Nathan.

Nick whispered to Hunt. "I thought you said they didn't meet on Friday nights?"

"They don't--this must be some kind of special event." Hunt peeked into the main room. "What should we do?"

"We gotta get out of here," Nick said uneasily.

"Let's just remain calm," whispered Nathan. "As long as they stay in there, they'll never see us."

"Stay until they leave?"

"I can't risk the chance of getting caught," replied Nathan.

Suddenly, a large commotion arose in the main room. Fifteen additional figures paraded into room, encircling the 15 students already seated at the table. These 15 members were dressed in long black robes that resembled Ku Klux Klan costumes. Some had animal skins draped around their robes. All their faces were covered by white hoods that had a skull and crossbones symbol stitched on the forehead. Each carried symbolic objects such as skulls, rainmaker sticks, and sculptures of the Illuminati eye. They danced around the room in a counterclockwise motion, shaking their objects and humming in deep voices.

The stiff movements of these robed figures made it clear that they were not college students--undoubtedly, they were long-time members of the society. Nathan whispered to Hunt and Nick. "This must be an initiation ceremony."

The robed figures stopped in place and started chanting in cold, deep voices. "The Truth equals death; the Devil equals death; Death equals death!" The figures repeated the chant five more times until one individual--the only figure wearing a red mask--climbed atop the table.

"Fellow Bonesmen, we are gathered here tonight to celebrate the initiation of new blood into the Brotherhood." He spread his arms out wide and addressed those at the table. "Younglings, welcome your bones into this society by drinking the blood of Bonesmen."

The 15 students reached for the fifteen decorated goblets situated on the table in front of them. The silver goblets resembled something taken from King Arthur's court. They brought the silver chalices to their lips and slowly began drinking the contents. Most had a hard time keeping the liquid in their mouths--their faces reflected their disgust.

"What's in those cups?" whispered Nick.

"Blood."

"Human blood?"

"No, I'm sure it's venison or cattle."

Many of the student Bonesmen looked nauseous. The older Bonesmen stood behind them, nodding their heads in approval.

The figure with the red hood once again gained everyone's attention. "The 15 of you are now a part of the Skull and Bones Brotherhood. The Brotherhood will be your Way to power. The Brotherhood will create the Truth. The Brotherhood will be your Life." The figure walked across the table to put his foot on the six-foot long wooden casket in the center. "Now, as your first act as Bonesmen, you must lie within the holy tomb and share your innermost experiences that entertained your flesh."

The first student climbed atop the table and got into the wooden casket situated in the center. He laid prostate in the casket while sharing his most intimate sexual experiences.

The three listened with disgust to one story after another of perverse sexual acts--sex acts with underage individuals, acts with individuals of the same sex, and even acts with animals.

After two hours, Nick was getting restless. "I can't take this anymore."

"At least they aren't doing what they used to do in that casket before they started allowing females to join."

"What was that?" asked Hunt, part of him not wanting to know.

"I'll spare the details, but basically orgies and group masturbation."

Nick, a good-natured kid who was fairly religious, was getting disgusted by listening to the occult rituals. "Let's get out of here. I don't know how much longer I can keep quiet."

Nathan looked at the single window in the corner. "You think we could crawl out that window without making any noise?"

Nick nodded.

As the Bonesmen licked their lips as one of the female member's recounting of her sexual experiences from the casket, Hunt, Nick, and Nathan tiptoed to the reading room's window. Nathan took hold of the window's lock and attempted to rotate it to the unlocked position. Although he moved it as slowly as possible, the lock resonated a loud screech at first movement. Obviously it had not been opened in years.

All eyes in the main room turned to the reading room's door. Several of the older Bonesmen started walking in that direction to investigate the noise.

"They're coming," said Hunt, unable to keep his voice to a whisper. "What should we do?"

Nick pushed up on the window sill. "Dad, you jump out first. I'll create a distraction if I have to."

"Nick, make sure you get out. There's no telling what they'll do to you."

"Go!" yelled Nick. "Don't worry about me."

Three Bonesmen entered the room. Nathan jumped headfirst out the window.

"They're heading out the windows. Stop them!"

Hunt immediately followed Nathan. The Bonesmen ran toward the window. Two of them grabbed Nick before he could make the jump. The other shut the window and locked it.

"Who are you?" demanded a voice behind the cloth mask.

Instead of answering, Nick stomped on his foot. As soon as he relinquished his grasp, Nick pushed away the other Bonesmen. Nick started to run.

"Make sure he doesn't get away!" said the Bonesman hopping on one foot. The two others immediately chased Nick into the main room.

Nick entered the main room where 27 others were awaiting him. They quickly encircled him, looking ready to attack. He had nowhere to go.

As the surrounding circle inched closer and closer, Nick grabbed one of the torches from its holder. He whisked it about, sending the Bonesmen backing away from the fire.

"Put it down, or you'll regret…" threatened the Bonesman in red.

Nick turned to face this figure who was blocking the entrance to the foyer. He stood knees bent, in a martial fighter's stance. "Regret what?"

"Nothing you'll be able to remember," he said with a bit of arrogance hidden in his voice.

Even though he could not see the figure's face, Nick knew the Bonesman had an evil grin behind that red mask from the thought of cruel punishment.

Without wasting any more time, Nick tossed the torch high in the air with the fire end flying toward the red Bonesman. The Bonesman's eyes focused on the small ball of fire as it flew directly at him. Instinctively, he sidestepped out of the way to avoid the flame.

As soon as the red Bonesman sidestepped, Nick ran toward the gap. He dove headfirst and slid across the wooden floor past the Bonesmen. He jumped up near the foyer and headed for the door.

"Grab him!" yelled one of them.

Several of the student Bonesmen followed him out the door. Nick, however, was too fast for these students dressed in their business suits. The three stopped chasing as soon as they realized they'd never catch him.

Nathan and Hunt waited for Nick at a corner that was well out of sight from the Bones Tomb. "What happened?" asked Hunt as Nick approached.

"Nothing," said Nick out of breath. "They got a good look at my face, but I was able to escape. Let's hurry up and get back to my place where it's safe."

"I can see why the Skull and Bones members have so much power," said Nick entering his apartment. "They basically sell their souls to the devil."

"You'd be surprised how many political and business leaders are involved with organizations closely tied to the occult," said Nathan. "There's also the Freemasons, the Bohemian Grove, and several others."

"Our national leaders are involved in stuff like that?" asked Hunt.

Nathan nodded. "In fact, that's what our president was doing when he was in college. Bush is supposedly a Christian now, but while he was studying at Yale, he was engaging in the occult rituals and orgies of Skull and Bones."

Nick was still traumatized from the episode. "I didn't like the feel of that place--it was like an eerie sense of evil."

"I think we'd better stay away from there awhile," said Nathan. "I'd like to see what they know and what's inside that chest, but it's not worth getting caught. Their possible connection to 9/11 is just a minor detail in the whole scheme of things. My report will mainly cover the massive amount of evidence that Daniel has already researched. I think it's important that I stick only to the facts that are backed up by solid evidence."

"Sounds like a good plan."

Chapter 37

Millard Station Apartments
October 6, 2006
11:15 p.m.

Over the next three weeks, Nathan worked non-stop on his report based on Daniel's research.

One night, Nick approached his closet door and knocked before entering. He found his father hunched over his laptop, looking over dozens of papers scattered on the floor.

"Dad, can I talk to you for a minute?"

Nathan's bloodshot eyes turned from the computer. He took a deep breath and ran his hand through his oily beard. "Sure, I could use a break." Nathan got up from the folding chair and tiptoed around the papers on the floor. Even though it looked like a scattered mess, the papers were actually carefully organized to allow Nathan to glean their information as he typed.

"What's on your mind?" asked Nathan, emerging from the closet.

Nick pointed down at all the printed papers in the closet. "I noticed that you're writing your report using only Daniel Lewin's information. Are you sure Daniel was someone you could trust?"

"I'm positive," replied Nathan, somewhat surprised with Nick's suggestion. "Daniel was a genius. He spent five years of his life hacking into computers and investigating this stuff."

"But what if he didn't? What if he didn't do all those things he told you? Or what if some of his evidence was false?"

"They're all based on documented research and reputable sources." Nathan picked up one of the papers from the closet. "For instance, this one came from the Pentagon--there's no doubt they're real."

"But what if he's left out part of the story?"

"What are you getting at?" said Nathan in a defensive tone.

"I've come across several sources on the Internet that say Israeli forces could've been involved in some aspect of 9/11. With Daniel's background as an Israeli special forces agent, I think he could've had a motivation to hide information that would point to an Israeli connection--he himself might have been involved in 9/11."

Nathan's patience was running low. "Nick, I don't have time to worry about outlandish 'what if...' possibilities."

"Outlandish?" replied Nick, slightly offended. "A bunch of people think Israel was somehow involved in 9/11. One website says that many Jews in New York were warned to stay away from the Twin Towers on 9/11 via a Jewish Instant Messenger service. Larry Silverstein, the owner of the Twin Towers, is close friends with former Israeli Prime Minister Benjamin Netanyahu. We should be looking into these things."

"I'm not going to waste my time looking into any anti-Semitic websites," said Nathan, raising his tone. "There are crazy racists all over the world who try to blame the Jews for everything."

"I'm not saying the Jews were behind 9/11. I just think that PNAC may have had help from Mossad. Mossad is like the Israeli CIA--they've had a long history of being involved in shady activities."

Nathan shook his head. "This isn't something we should be worried about."

"How do you know? How do you know that Daniel wasn't misleading you?"

"I just know!" Nathan snapped back. The tone of his voice grew sharper as his temper grew. "I've got a hundred things running around my mind right now. The last thing I need is you bothering me about whether we can trust our information."

"It's just that…"

"Just give it up!"

"No! This is something we've got to set straight."

"Fine. If you want to waste your time reading neo-Nazi websites, go ahead. But I'm going to finish my report using the sources that I know are fact." Nathan stormed to the closet, slamming the door behind him.

Nathan got back on his computer and tried starting where he left off. But it was no use--his emotions prevented him from thinking straight. For an hour, he thought about what Nick had said. He realized he had acted childishly in the argument and needed to apologize.

Nathan walked into the living room and saw Nick and Jay doing homework. "Nick, can I have a word with you?"

Nick followed his father to the bedroom.

Nathan took a deep breath. "I just wanted to apologize for the way I acted a little while ago. The combination of getting less than four hours of sleep a night and the stress of completing this report has put me in a testy mood."

"That's fine--I know you're under a lot of pressure. I'm just worried that Daniel Lewin may not have told you the complete truth."

"That's a valid concern. But I'm sure Daniel was not trying to protect himself or any of his Israeli friends." Nathan looked across the room and saw Nick's Bible on a nightstand beside his bed. "Nick, you believe that there's a God. You can't see Him or prove His existence, but you have faith that He is real. The same is true for what Daniel told me. I can't prove that Daniel wasn't misleading me, but something inside of me tells me that Daniel was sharing the complete truth. You get what I'm saying?"

"Yeah, I understand."

"I just feel that this idea of researching an Israeli connection would be a distraction for us right now. There's a chance that certain Israeli citizens may be connected in a minor way. But I'm not focusing on the minor details. I'm focusing my report on the facts that prove PNAC and other top officials in Washington were the main perpetrators that planned and executed 9/11. Once I expose these major issues, I believe the floodwaters will break and all the minor details will come to surface on their own."

"I guess I agree with you."

Nathan was able to tell that Nick was not completely satisfied with his answer. "If you want to investigate more into an Israeli connection, I'll try to add any credible evidence that you find to my report."

"Yeah, I think I'll do that. Tomorrow is Saturday--I'll plan on taking most of the day to research."

Nathan smiled. "You know, I'm glad we had that argument tonight. From now on, we need to make sure we're both on the same page. Once this report comes out, there's going to be a lot of opposition that we'll face. We can't let petty differences distract us from telling others the truth."

Nathan went to bed shortly after his conversation with Nick.

After getting a good night's rest, he used the next day to work tirelessly on his report. Throughout the day he only took two breaks, one to use the restroom and one to get something to eat and drink.

He looked over his report. It was already 400 pages, and there was still more information that needed to be added. He looked down at his watch; he could not believe it was already 11:00 p.m.

Nathan took a break to see how Nick's research went. He walked into the living room and found Jay sitting in front of his laptop, but Nick was nowhere in sight.

"Where's Nick?"

Jay shrugged. "Haven't seen him all day. He wasn't here last night when I went to bed. I thought maybe you told him to go somewhere for the weekend."

Nathan shook his head, concerned. "The last time I talked to him was around nine o'clock last night. He said he was going to spend all day researching."

Nathan tried calling Nick from his Blackberry, but there was no answer. Over the next two hours, he left several voice messages, getting increasingly worried each time.

Finally, just before 3:00 a.m., Nick walked through the door. His jeans were ripped, his face swollen and cut.

"Nick! What happened?" Nathan was already on his feet.

Nick nonchalantly replied. "I'm fine."

"You hardly look fine. What happened?"

He walked to his bedroom, not paying much attention to the fact his father had stayed up for him.

"Let's just say that I've been busy researching." Nick flopped down onto his bed.

"Researching?" asked Nathan.

"You were right--the sites that promote an Israeli connection are run by anti-Semitic racists--or disinformation agents working for the government that try to give 9/11 Truth a bad name." said Nick in a half-asleep state. "But I did find something else that was very interesting."

"What was it? And why do you look like that?"

"Let me get some sleep, and I'll tell you about it tomorrow morning." Nick grabbed his pillow and put it up to his bloody face. "Better yet, make that tomorrow afternoon.

"Nick, are you in trouble? Tell me what happened!"

It was too late. He was already asleep.

**To learn about Nick's eventful day, please visit the book's website at: www.AmTruth.com

Chapter 38

Millard Station Apartments
October 13, 2006
9:11 a.m.

Nathan walked into the living room with a smile on his face. A pair of Ray-Bans could not hide the light in his eyes. "It's done. It took me 550 pages and a little over three weeks, but my report exposing the truth about 9/11 is finally done."

"Everything is happening at perfect timing," said Nick. "As of last night, we have over 5,000 members in our '9/11 Cover-Up' group on Facebook. I'll be able to post a message to tell all these people about the report. "

"And I've compiled a list of over a hundred press members in addition to the media contacts you already know," said Hunt. "We can send your report by email, and these journalists could have a story on it by the end of this week."

"And I plan on taking all of next week to make phone calls to follow up with these media contacts," said Joseph. "I'll make sure they read the report, and I'll make sure they run a story on it."

"I have a list of 1,000 Truth Movement advocates," said Jay. "So even if the mainstream media does not cover this at first, we'll have 1,000 dedicated individuals who will make sure that the truth will fall into the right hands. Many on the list have their own 9/11 Truth websites or radio talk shows."

"And me and Jay started filming the video presentation of the 9/11 facts." Nick picked up the professional movie camera they had rented from the campus media library. "I think it will present a powerful message that will open up a lot of eyes."

Nathan smiled with satisfaction. "Guys, I can't thank you enough. I think we'll look back and see this as the day that changed this nation's history—"

The sharp ring of a phone interrupted Nathan. All four college students knew that the sound did not match their personalized ringtones.

"Whose phone is that?" asked Jay.

All of them looked into Nick's bedroom, where the noise was coming from. They went into the bedroom and discovered it was Nathan's Blackberry.

"Nobody has this number," said Nathan, with a concerned tone. He picked up the phone and detached the power cord that was charging it.

"A wrong number?"

Nathan looked at the familiar number on the caller ID. "This is Robert Montgomery's number. But how could—"

"Uncle Robert?" interrupted Nick.

"Who?"

"Robert is one of my close friends at the Pentagon. I was going to send the report to him later today--he works in communications and has plenty of media contacts."

Nathan's phone beeped, alerting him that he had a new message. He checked his voicemail:

"Nathan, you've got to leave immediately! Federal agents are tracking this mobile phone and are on their way. I don't know what's exactly going on, but I hope I can get you out of this. I'm on my way now."

Nathan darted to the living room. The look in his eyes told the other four the seriousness of the situation. "We've got to send everything immediately. Hunt, do you have the email lists with you?"

"No, they're on my computer in my dorm."

"Get them now! We need to email my report ASAP. I'm also going to need two copies of the report printed." Nathan pulled a memory chip off his key ring and handed it to Joseph. "Joseph, you and Jay go to the copy center and run two copies."

As the others rushed out the door, Nathan turned to his son. "Nick, fill the car full of gas and have it ready to leave here in fifteen minutes."

Nick started for the door.

"Nick, hold up." Nathan tossed the Blackberry to his son. "Take my cell phone and put it on a bus at the bus stop."

Nick examined the sense of worry in his father's eyes. "Dad, what's happening?"

"I'll fill you in as soon as you get back. There's no time now."

As soon as he left, Nathan grabbed a piece of paper, wrote a short note, and stuffed it inside a stamped envelope. Nathan ran to the mailbox at the apartment complex and mailed the letter. Even though his adrenaline was pumping, he grew winded over the short distance--it had been a couple weeks since he had done any physical activity.

As he rounded the corner to the apartment building, he saw a black Crown Victoria speeding from the other direction. His loss of breath faded from his mind when he saw the federal agent's car. He sprinted to the staircase to the apartment. He had to get to a phone to warn Nick and his friends not to come back.

The car squealed to a stop just in front of the apartment's staircase. Malum jumped out of the car, gun drawn. "Stop right there!"

Nathan threw the door open and locked the deadbolt.

Seconds later, he heard agent Malum running up the stairs. Nathan tried to clear his head.

Malum pounded on the door. "Open up!"

Nathan gasped for air as he tried to come up with a plan for a way out.

Agent Malum took a few steps back and kicked the door. The deadbolt was no match for his strength. Malum stormed in. "Freeze! Don't move!"

Nathan put his hands in the air.

"It was quite the clever trick you just pulled--putting your cell phone in someone else's car. The rest of my team is chasing after that vehicle right now." Malum scanned the room as he inched closer to Nathan. "I have to say--you found a clever hiding spot. But calling your son four times in one night? You're smarter than that, Mr. Alexander." Malum kicked open some of the notebooks lying on the floor as he kept his gun pointed at Nathan. "Where's your information?"

Nathan remained silent.

The agent pointed the gun closer to Nathan. "Where *is* it, Mr. Alexander!"

"You can kill me. I'll gladly die defending the truth. But even if you kill me now, it won't make a difference. My research is going out to others as we speak."

"Don't worry. We're going to kill you. We may even let hundreds of rats eat you alive." Nathan's spine tingled at the thought of rats chewing away at his flesh. "But first, we're going to make sure that information gets nowhere. So where is it?"

"I'll never tell you anything."

Malum took out his cell phone and punched in a number. "Put her on," he said when the other line picked up. Malum pressed the phone to Nathan's ear.

"Daddy?"

"Claire! Are you all right?"

Crying, she managed to say, "They have a gun pointed at my head."

Malum yanked the phone away from Nathan's ear. "Tell us where you're keeping the information, or your daughter dies."

"I don't have it. It's with someone else."

"Who?"

Jay and Joseph had the only physical piece of his report besides what was saved on his computer. Nathan remained silent, trying to stall.

"I'll give you to the count of three before she suffers. *One.*"

Nathan shook his head. "This isn't right."

"*TWO—*"

"Stop! I'll tell you!"

As soon as these words exited Nathan's mouth, Nick burst into the room. Before either of the two knew what was happening, Nick kicked Malum's elbow, grabbed his wrist, and used the back of his left hand to slap away the gun. The gun flew across the room and landed in the corner. Malum backhanded Nick off him, sending him to the floor.

Both Nathan and Malum eyed the weapon for a brief moment, then dove for it.

They slid to the ground and bumped heads as they reached for the pistol. Their hands grabbed it simultaneously. They wrestled on the floor, trying to gain control of the weapon.

Nick got up and ran to help his father. However, Malum's strength quickly ripped the gun from Nathan's grasp.

Malum pointed the gun at the approaching Nick. "Hands up in the air!" Nick froze--focused on the gun a few feet from him.

Malum stood and grabbed Nick's shoulder, backing him away from Nathan in the corner. He pressed the barrel of the pistol to the back of Nick's head. With his other hand, he took out his phone. "Frank, hold off on hurting the girl just yet. We can save her for the future. Something just as good walked in the door."

Malum closed the phone. He shoved the gun harder into Nick's skull, causing Nick's neck to tilt forward. "Where is it?"

Nathan got up to his feet. "I'll give you the information, just don't—"

"No, Dad."

Nathan stared into his son's eyes. A period of silence followed. "No one else has the information. It's all in the bedroom--in my laptop and two notebooks."

Malum eyed the bedroom. He pushed Nick forward to lead him in that direction. As soon as Malum lowered his guard to walk toward the bedroom, Nick reached into his pocket and drove his grandfather's knife into Malum's side.

Before the stunned agent realized a six-inch Navy SEAL knife was lodged in his abdomen, Nick sent the back of his elbow into Malum's throat. Nick continued with a martial arts combo in which he kicked the gun from Malum's hand.

Nathan ran toward the two. He cocked back his fist and threw a punch that landed between Malum's eyes. Malum fell to the floor, unconscious.

Nick eyed the fallen agent. The wound in his side was slowly bleeding, but it was not serious. "What do we do with him?"

"No time to deal with him. We got to get out of here."

"The car's waiting."

"I still need time to get all my stuff together. While I'm doing this, pick up Jay and Joseph from the copy center. Same with Hunt. Then meet me back here, but don't come in the main entrance. Meet me on the highway that runs behind the apartment complex."

Nick raced out the door, calling his friends to find their locations.

Nathan dropped to a knee and dug through Malum's pocket to find the agent's cell phone. As he examined Malum's wound closer, he knew the minor injury would not hinder the trained agent once he came back to his senses.

He opened Malum's phone and searched for the number of the last call. After memorizing the nine-digit number, he used the phone to call someone he could trust.

"Washington D.C. police. Donna Madden speaking."

"I need you to direct me to Mike Savage in the detective's unit."

"May I ask who this—"

"My daughter's life is on the line! I need to speak to Sergeant Savage immediately!"

The secretary immediately forwarded the call.

"Savage."

"Mike, it's Nathan. My daughter has been kidnapped. I need you to run a trace for a cell phone. The number is 551-122-1963."

Savage scrambled to find a pen. "Nathan, what's going on?"

"Have there been any rumors about me floating around the station?"

"No. Why?"

"I'll explain it to you later. Just use that number to find my daughter."

"Will do."

Savage was a close friend who had been Nathan's next door neighbor since they had moved into their house on Fourth Street in the fall of '97. Nathan prayed that he'd be able to find his daughter before anything serious happened.

Nathan grabbed Nick's backpack from the table and dumped everything out. He stepped over Malum and went into the bedroom. He frantically stuffed his notebooks, files, and laptop in the backpack. He scanned the closet, making sure he got everything. Nathan tossed the backpack over his shoulder and left the apartment.

As Nathan ran down the stairs, he saw a familiar figure coming across the parking lot. Robert.

Robert ran up to his friend. "Nathan, thank God I found you. You're in trouble."

Nathan didn't pause. "I know." He walked toward the rear of the apartment as fast as his pace would allow. Robert followed Nathan closely behind. "I've already run into someone who's supposedly with the FBI. Robert, do you know what's going on?"

"At the Pentagon, they told a select number of us that you're stealing government information and selling it to terrorists."

"Trust me; that couldn't be further from the truth."

"I know. That's why I sent you the warning. The rumor going around is that you know something about 9/11."

"More than something," said Nathan, pacing through the woods to the highway. "I wrote a 550-page report exposing how certain government authorities planned and executed 9/11."

"Will you let me see it?"

"You're on my list. I'm having someone make you a copy as we speak. With your media contacts and the clout you have at the Pentagon, I'm counting on you to help me expose the truth."

"I'll deliver this report to everyone I know. Is that all the information you have?"

Nathan stepped over a patch of thorns that had grown over the path leading into the woods. "Pretty much, except for the notebooks in this backpack and what's on my laptop."

Robert tightly grabbed Nathan by his bicep and turned him around to face him. Nathan noticed that Robert now had a black glove on his right hand. With this hand, he took out a gun from his waist and pointed it at Nathan.

"Robert, what are you doing?"

Robert lowered his weapon and fired two shots into Nathan's knee caps.

Nathan fell to the ground. He quickly used his arms to pick himself up where he was upright on his knees, facing Robert. "Why? Why are *you* doing this?"

"I've been in on this since the day after 9/11. They approached me when I started asking questions about smelling cordite. They needed me to help them do what was best for this country." Robert spoke with an aggression that Nathan had never heard from him before. "There are just some things that people do not deserve to know."

"I thought I could trust you!"

"Just like the American public thought they could trust the reports we wrote on 9/11."

Robert knelt down and put the barrel to Nathan's temple. "Make this easy for me, Nathan."

Even though it was not his nature to go down without a fight, Nathan made no attempt to flee. He simply stared into the eyes of his thought-to-be friend. "Just promise me that nothing will happen to Nick or Claire."

Robert gave a solemn nod. He then grabbed Nathan's wrist and forced his finger to pull the trigger.

Nathan's body collapsed as the bullet entered his skull. Nathan's head fell to the side of his unwounded temple, making his face visible to Robert. His mouth gaped open, as if it were displaying the ultimate sense of betrayal.

Robert stood motionless. The sight brought a deep sense of pain and regret over his soul. But he eventually rationalized that it was just business. Regardless of his personal connections with this man, it was his duty to get rid of this threat. "You ought to be thankful I got to you first," he said, walking over to the backpack. "If those agents got a hold of you, they'd be torturing you as we speak."

He took one last look at Nathan and decided that he'd at least stick to his word in making sure Nick and Claire would be all right. He picked up the backpack and left Nathan lying in the woods.

Chapter 39

The White House - Oval Office
October 13, 2006
3:22 p.m.

President Bush sat at his desk reading a briefing on the war in Iraq. His chief of staff entered. "Sir, you have a phone call. It's one of your advisors."

President Bush took the phone. "Hello."

"George, it's Wolfowitz."

The president sat up straight and listened intently to his distinguished friend.

"I've just been informed that our problem has been taken care of."

"When?"

"Just a couple hours ago," said Wolfowitz. "They found him at his son's apartment."

"Was it your man from the FBI who found him?"

"No, it was actually one of my men working in Communications Department at the Pentagon--the one who has helped us in influencing the media."

"Make sure you give this man a promotion with a nice title and pay raise."

"Yes, sir."

"Thanks for the news, Paul. I look forward to telling my dad."

"Not a problem."

Bush hung up and handed the phone back to his chief of staff. "It looks like our little secret will stay a secret after all." Bush looked down at his desk as a sense of worry folded across his eyes. "But has it been worth all this?"

"Of course, sir. It has successfully taken care of a potential oil crisis and elevated this country to an even greater world power. It was the decision any good president would make."

Bush examined the papers on his desk that showed his low approval ratings in the most recent polls. *It was a decision any* **good** *president would make,* Bush repeated to himself. The worry on his face slowly turned into a smug grin.

At the same time in another part of Washington, an even wider grin appeared on Wolfowitz's face. *That idiot. He doesn't even know he's being used like a puppet.*

Chapter 40

Millard Station Apartments
October 13, 2006
3:33 p.m.

Nick watched a team of FBI agents haul everything from his apartment. They literally tore up the place in their search for any possible evidence Nathan might have left behind. They confiscated all of Nick's textbooks and school notebooks, considering the possibility that that they may have some communication in them.

A man with a limp came out from the bedroom, carrying a small leather wallet. He flipped open the wallet to reveal an FBI badge that had his identity on it. "I never thought I'd get this back," said Agent Stephens.

Hunt and Joseph showed up at the apartment. Nick went over to talk to them as the agents went through the rest of his stuff. "They take all of your stuff, too?"

"All of it," said Hunt. "They took my laptop and won't give it back."

"They even took some of the computers in the library," said Joseph.

"All our media contacts, the list of Truth Advocates-- gone."

Nick walked over to one of the FBI agents. "Excuse me, sir. I have a question."

"Yes…"

"How did my dad die?"

"That hasn't been disclosed to us. We're just here to gather the evidence."

Nick approached another agent who had stored the Navy SEAL knife in a clear Ziploc bag. "Is there any way I could get that knife back in the future? It's a family heirloom."

As Nick said this, Malum walked by, carrying a small bag in the hand opposite the side of his stab wound. He said nothing, but glared fiercely into Nick's eyes. Nick stared right back, taking notice of the dark black circles around Malum's eyes that were the evidence of his father's punch. As Malum walked past, Nick continued his death stare into the back of his shiny bald head.

The FBI agent raised the clear packaging to eye level to draw Nick's attention back to the knife. The agent checked to make sure the cap at the bottom could not unscrew. "You'll get the knife back as soon as we process it."

The door to the apartment flung open. "NICK."

Nick turned to see who it was. It was Robert.

Seeing his dad's best friend brought back so many memories. The sight immediately brought tears to his eyes.

Seeing Nick's emotions made Robert start weeping as well. He embraced Nick, letting Nick pour his grief onto his shoulder. "I was the one that had to tell your father about Cindy." Robert's emotions dramatically slowed his speech. "Now, I've got to be the one to tell you about your father."

"How did it happen?"

"I've been told he committed suicide--a gunshot wound to the head." Robert paused and glared at one of the FBI agents. "But that's *their* story." He then whispered in Nick's ear, "Hopefully you can tell me what's really going on."

Two days later, Nick sat alone in the campus cafeteria. He spent nearly two hours reflecting on memories of his dad as he attempted to eat a sandwich. Nick tried to remain strong about it, but there was no way to hide a broken heart. He could not even be around the other three--they only reminded him of his dad and their shattered dream of telling the world the truth.

Nick examined the small wound in his right wrist. Before leaving, the FBI had implanted a computer chip into his arm that allowed them to track him at all times. *I guess everyone will receive one of these chips in the future, when our tyrannical government gains complete control.*

Nick grew even more depressed as he thought about how the American public was blind at seeing how their freedom was being stripped away.

Walking back to his apartment, Nick called Claire to make sure she was doing alright. She recalled being kidnapped, but she remembered nothing else. She had obviously been drugged. She was now at Granny Mia's house. Nick was comforted by the fact that Robert had promised to check up on her as much as he could. Nick decided to wait until he saw her in person to tell her what had really happened.

Before going back to his apartment, Nick checked his mail. Inside the mailbox was a thick white envelope. It had no return address, but was written in handwriting that he immediately recognized. Nick took his grandfather's Navy SEAL knife from his pocket and used it to open the envelope.

Inside the envelope was a sheet of paper folded around a black leather case. Nick opened the thin case and discovered it was Malum's FBI badge. He read the letter, which was in his father's handwriting.

Nick,

My life is in immediate danger. Hopefully when you get this I'll be alive and well, and we'll be in the process of distributing my report to media outlets. If not, I wanted to leave the truth behind to the only person I can trust. At the below email address, you will find my 550-page report, plus all of Daniel Lewin's research.

T.Ruth.Moore@gmail.com
Password: 911Truth

Nick folded the letter and put it into his pocket alongside the FBI identification badge. Nick took a moment to think of his father, then tilted his head to the heavens. "I promise, Dad. I *will* tell the world the truth."

What Now...

Writing a book on a controversial topic about a tragedy that has had an effect all over the world, I tried my best to write in an unbiased and nonpartisan manner. I do not have anything against the Bush administration, nor am I anti-American in any way. I do not have any personal ties to the 9/11 tragedy, other than the fact that I regard 9/11 as a deliberate attack against my fellow Americans and my nation's freedom (regardless of who was actually behind the attacks). I did not write this book with a hidden agenda--from the beginning, all I have wanted is the truth.

If you're also curious about the truth surrounding the 9/11 tragedy, I encourage you to do some researching on your own. There's a large amount of information that is not covered in this book (However, some of the 9/11 Truth issues are based on bad information, some of which may or may not be supplied by government agents working on a disinformation campaign). On the www.AmTruth.com website, I've given you access to many web links, films/documentaries, and other sources of free information that are from credible sources.

If you agree with me in that we do not the truth about 9/11, I encourage you to help bring this issue to the public's attention. Here's a simple action plan on how we can make this happen:

1. **Do whatever you're good at.** I'm a writer, so I wrote a story that helped people think about 9/11 from a different perspective. If you're a musician, write a song about 9/11 Truth. If you're popular, start a conversation about 9/11 Truth with everyone you know at a party. If you're a good cook, invite friends and neighbors over for a dinner and try to start a conversation at the dinner table. If you have an email mailing list, write a brief email to your colleagues and friends.

2. **Inform your elected representatives.** Whether on the city, state, or national levels, we need to make sure our Congressmen and elected officials are aware of this serious issue.

3. **If you are the praying type – pray.** Though 9/11 Truth is predominately a political issue, it is not an issue that should be strictly dealt within the political realm. Nearly every religion has a desire to interpret the truth of life, and considering the amount of religious blame that has been associated with 9/11, I think this is an issue that organized religion and religious groups should help promote.

4. **Network with others**. Make connections and friendships with others in your local area who share an interest in 9/11 Truth. If your community has not established a local 9/11 Truth group/committee, start your own--or find a virtual community on the Internet. Whatever ways you can contribute to the 9/11 Truth Movement, you'll always be able to accomplish more with the help of a group or friends.

Acknowledgements

I have to thank certain individuals and groups who helped with this book:

1. Mr. Ken Kennedy
I can't thank you enough for contributing several 9/11 Truth facts that only a select few know about. Your hard-nose investigation into 9/11 inspired the ideas and plot structure of this book.

2. The 9/11 Truth Movement
I could not have written this book without all the research conducted by the individuals committed to 9/11 Truth. In particular, I would like to thank Dr. Steven E. Jones, Dr. David Ray Griffin, and Jim Hoffman for the excellent research they've done. I want to give special thanks to others who are spreading the word about 9/11 Truth issues:

- Michael Wosely in hosting the *Visibility 9/11* Podcast,
- dc9/11truth – for their numerous websites, events, and activist campaigns,
- *Loose Change* Crew – for their awesome film that puts a thought-provoking, and sometimes humorous, perspective on the controversies of 9/11.

3. Alex Jones
I have to especially thank Alex Jones for his commitment to exposing the truth. I admit that some of his views come

across as being radical, but I still want to acknowledge the great work he's doing for the 9/11 Truth Movement. He was actually a "prophet" for 9/11 Truth in that he accurately predicted the attacks before September 2001. Since then, his radio program and documentaries have aggressively informed others about 9/11 truth and related New World Order issues.

4. Editors
I have to thank the team that helped me with editing and proofreading this work. Nancy Hill helped me make this work read more like a novel rather than a presentation of 9/11 Truth facts. Ian Woods from Global Outlook Magazine and Matt Sullivan of The Rock Creek Free Press did an excellent job in spotting the grammar mistakes, as well as making sure my ideas were backed by credible information.

5. Friends and Family
For those who supported my anti-social lifestyle during the months of writing this book. I spent nearly all my free time writing/researching and was unable to spend too much quality time with those who've always been there for me. In the future, I hope to spend more time with all of you and to enjoy living life in the greatest nation in the world.

Sources for "The Facts"

The following are sources for the information presented in the introductory nonfiction section. Instead of using these long web urls, I suggest you go to the **www.AmTruth.com** website and click on the link "The Facts." In addition to being able to click on all these urls, I have provided videos, images, maps, and other interactive media on the website to give you more information.

Also on the website are sources for some of the information I presented in the novel.

36
http://en.wikipedia.org/wiki/9/11_conspiracy_theories
http://www.time.com/time/magazine/article/0,9171,1531304,00.html [1]
http://www.angus-reid.com/polls/index.cfm/fuseaction/viewItem/
itemID/13469 [2]
http://www.zogby.com/search/ReadNews.dbm?ID=855 [3]

Controlled Demolition Theory
http://www.scrippsnews.com/911poll
http://en.wikipedia.org/wiki/Controlled_demolition_hypothesis_
for_the_collapse_of_the_World_Trade_Center

Squibs
http://911research.wtc7.net/wtc/analysis/collapses/squibs.html

3 Weeks
http://911research.wtc7.net/wtc/evidence/moltensteel.htm
http://infowars.net/articles/november2006/171106molten.htm
Videos and PowerPoints: (see www.AmTruth.com website)

Over 50
http://911research.wtc7.net/wtc/evidence/oralhistories/explosions.html
http://www.911truth.org/article.php?story=20060118104223192
http://bellaciao.org/en/article.php3?id_article=6625
Video: (See Online)

7 Seconds
http://www.wtc7.net/

300 feet
http://911research.wtc7.net/wtc/evidence/photos/wtc7pile.html
http://en.wikipedia.org/wiki/7_World_Trade_Center
Map: (See Online)

3
http://www.wtc7.net/buildingfires.html
http://physics911.net/closerlook.htm
http://www.lewrockwell.com/reynolds/reynolds12.html

32
http://911research.wtc7.net/sept11/transactions.html
http://www.informationliberation.com/index.php?id=15459

$124 Million
http://www.informationliberation.com/index.php?id=15459
http://www.whatreallyhappened.com/cutter.html

2,626
http://www.gatago.com/alt/true-crime/5368505.html
http://colorado.indymedia.org/newswire/display/12797/index.
php

"Pull It"
http://www.whatreallyhappened.com/wtc7.html
http://www.prisonplanet.com/011904wtc7.html

8:46 a.m.
http://www.cooperativeresearch.org/essay.jsp?article=essayanint
erestingday
http://www.whatreallyhappened.com/schoolvideo.html
http://www.911timeline.net/

9:05 a.m.
http://www.thenation.com/doc/20031006/alterman

6:00 a.m.
http://www.longboatobserver.com/showarticle.asp?ai=2172
http://www.prisonplanet.com/bush_and_atta_visit_same_resort_
in_the_hours_leading_to_911.htm
http://www.911timeline.net/

John P. O'Neill
http://en.wikipedia.org/wiki/John_P._O'Neill
http://www.pbs.org/wgbh/pages/frontline/shows/knew/
http://www.attackonamerica.net/themysterysurroundingthedeath
ofjohnoneill.htm

Daniel Lewin
http://en.wikipedia.org/wiki/Daniel_M._Lewin
http://en.wikipedia.org/wiki/Sayeret_Matkal
http://www.cooperativeresearch.org/entity.jsp?entity=daniel_lewin
http://www.akamai.com/html/industry/public_sector.html

Mahmoud Ahmad
http://en.wikipedia.org/wiki/Mahmoud_Ahmad
http://www.globalresearch.ca/articles/SCO410A.html
http://www.media-criticism.com/Mysteries_911_2002.html

Securacom
http://www.whatreallyhappened.com/911security.html
http://en.wikipedia.org/wiki/Securacom
http://www.commondreams.org/views04/0111-01.htm

September 10, 2001
http://www.cooperativeresearch.org/entity.jsp?entity=carlyle_
group

Asia
http://911research.wtc7.net/wtc/groundzero/cleanup.html
http://www.sourcewatch.org/index.php?title=Destruction_of_
Evidence_from_Ground_Zero_at_the_World_Trade_Center

Over 1 billion
http://www.pentagonstrike.co.uk/

Zero
http://911research.wtc7.net/pentagon/evidence/footage.html
http://911review.org/Wiki/PentagonAttack.shtml

44 feet 6 inches
http://physics911.net/missingwings.htm
http://www.kasjo.net/ats/Above_Top_Secret_article_1.htm
http://membres.lycos.fr/applemacintosh/pentagon.htm

1 inch
http://www.whatreallyhappened.com/hanjour.html
http://en.wikipedia.org/wiki/Hani_Hanjour
http://www.kasjo.net/ats/Above_Top_Secret_article_1.htm

Four
http://thewebfairy.com/killtown/flight77/lawn.html
www.serendipity.li/wot/crash_site.htm

63
http://911exposed.org/DNA.htm
http://thewebfairy.com/killtown/flight77/passengers.html

Charles Burlingame
http://en.wikipedia.org/wiki/Charles_Burlingame
http://www.pentagonresearch.com/101.html

25,000
http://pentagonresearch.com/pentagon.html
http://www.whs.pentagon.mil/work_pent.cfm

Operation Northwoods
http://en.wikipedia.org/wiki/Operation_Northwoods
http://www.wanttoknow.info/010501operationnorthwoods
http://www.whatreallyhappened.com/northwoods.html

PNAC
http://en.wikipedia.org/wiki/PNAC
http://www.oldamericancentury.org/pnac.htm

6 weeks
http://en.wikipedia.org/wiki/USA_PATRIOT_Act
http://www.duncanentertainment.com/patriotact.php

$2.5 million
http://911research.wtc7.net/sept11/stockputs.html
http://www.sfgate.com/cgi-bin/article.cgi?file=/chronicle/
archive/2001/09/29/MN186128.DTL
http://cnnstudentnews.cnn.com/2001/WORLD/europe/09/24/
gen.europe.shortselling/

$46 billion
http://killtown.911review.org/buffett.html
http://www.911timeline.net/
http://en.wikipedia.org/wiki/Warren_Buffet

2nd Largest Oil Reserves
http://www.globalpolicy.org/security/oil/irqindx.htm

Zero
http://911research.wtc7.net/planes/analysis/norad/index.html
http://www.911truth.org/article.php?story=20040731213239607

11 miles
http://www.cooperativeresearch.org/entity.jsp?entity=andrews_
air_force_base

2.3 trillion
http://911research.wtc7.net/sept11/trillions.html
http://www.cbsnews.com/stories/2002/01/29/eveningnews/
main325985.shtml

[1] Based on the monthly price to sponsor a child in the World Vision
program.
[2] Based on the retail prices of: LG VX8300 cell phone $99.99 +
iPod Shuffle 79.99 + Sony PS2 $129.99 + Sylvania 5" Portable TV
set 30.49 + *The American Truth* $9.99 = $355.95 x 6,556,000,000
people = $2.3 Trillion.
[3] Based on Forbes 2006 Top Ten Richest : Gates $46 billion +
Buffet $36 billion + Prince Alwaleed Bin Talal Alsaud 23.7 billion
+ Paul Allen $22 billion + Walton family 20.5 billion multiplied
by 5 + Karl Albrecht 18.5 = 226.7 billion multiplied by 10 = $2.28
trillion.

What did you think of *The American Truth*?

I'd love to hear you what your thoughts of this book. I even want to hear comments from those who have a negative view of some of the ideas I presented. I especially want to hear from you if this book made you question what's really going in the world today.

Please visit www.AmTruth.com for updates and more information.

Thanks,
Nick Shelton
Nick@AmTruth.com
August 12, 2007

Printed in the United States
222051BV00001B/11/A